THE LITTLE BOOK OF DARK TALES

© 2012

W. R. ARMSTRONG

Artwork © W. R. Armstrong, 2012

Grosvenor House
Publishing Limited

This book is published by
Grosvenor House Publishing Ltd
28-30 High Street, Guildford, Surrey, GU1 3EL.
www.grosvenorhousepublishing.co.uk

A CIP record for this book
is available from the British Library

ISBN 978-1-908596-44-4

ABOUT THE AUTHOR

W R Armstrong is married and lives in Staffordshire. He writes mainly for the supernatural horror market. His short stories have appeared in magazines such as *Writers' Forum* and *First Edition*. *The Little Book of Dark Tales* is a compilation of his short stories. His novels, *Hell Pit*, *A Cry From Beyond*, and *Bark at the Moon*, can be purchased as e-books from the Kindle store at Amazon.co.uk. His website can be found at www.wrarmstrong.com

CONTENTS

THE HELP CLINIC

"Where is this place? What am I doing here?"

"That's what they all ask," said the man sitting opposite Scott Markham. "Perfectly natural I suppose, given the circumstances." Glancing at the mass of unfinished paperwork lying on his desk, he added, "Please, allow me to sign off this little lot and you'll have my undivided attention, I promise."

Scott sat there twiddling his thumbs, feeling confused and frustrated. He wanted to get up and walk out, but something stopped him: the uncertainty of his situation maybe. He hadn't the foggiest idea what was going on. As a result, he felt like a lost child who's wandered unwittingly into an alien world where nothing and no one makes any sense. It was a scary feeling.

He'd just been called into the cramped office from the waiting area outside, presumably by the man in front of him, having spent the best part of God knows how long hanging around. And that was part of the problem, he really didn't have a clue exactly how long he'd been there; it appeared he'd lost track of time since entering the place. It was all so confusing. He cast his mind back to the moment he'd left the house that morning—sunny, he recalled it had been sunny—not surprising really, it was the middle of July, after all. As he'd reached the end of the garden path and stepped onto the pavement, he looked back over his shoulder and waved. Candice, framed in the doorway, waved back, smiling, looking lovely as usual: he was a very lucky man. What she saw in him, he really didn't know. Short, stocky and balding with a noticeable paunch and not yet forty, he should be ashamed: get down the gym; get fit before it's too late, he was forever urging himself.

Trouble was, the conviction was lacking. Still, no one is perfect. Besides, Candice, she loved him despite his obvious faults, as did Gemma, his daughter, just turned three, a bit of a handful but beautiful all the same. Just like her mother. Yep, he was a lucky man all right. Gorgeous family, decent little job working in local government (the pay was crap, but the hours and conditions were good), nice tidy house, he had a lot to be thankful for.

So why had he gone and done it?

Stupid, he'd been so stupid, getting himself mixed up with Jonas like he had, but he was desperate to get rid of the debt. It was so damn easy to get in over your head nowadays. So many people fell for the advertising bullshit they heard on the television and the radio and that came through the letterbox. Credit cards, bank loans, equity release schemes: so many varied and wonderful ways to get into deep water.

Once upon a time, he'd been able to exercise control, limiting himself to the occasional flutter on the horses, a couple of quid here and there, and the odd lottery ticket or scratch card, but that was all. He'd never been what you could call a serious punter. But that all started to change when he'd got hooked on the internet. The internet was to blame for his predicament, he was certain. If it wasn't for that, he'd still be a small-time player, but it made it so damn easy: gambling sites were everywhere, and they promised such huge rewards. The temptation was too great and he'd succumbed and got in way over his fat, balding head.

Christ, it didn't even seem like real money he was losing, it was like Monopoly money, so he'd carried on hoping to get lucky and win back what he'd lost, but the debt only got worse and he ended up getting banned from site after site. But so what, he'd thought, there were plenty more out there in cyber space.

Only it wasn't that easy, as he'd soon discovered: the sites you owed money to didn't simply disappear when they barred you from accessing them; they didn't forget the debt and wipe the slate clean—hell no, they did what every other creditor did, they went after the debtor baying for blood. Pretty soon the demands started flooding in, in the form of e-mails and official warning letters, followed by unpleasant phone calls. Then came the final straw: court papers and threats of a visit from the bailiffs. What an awful, stinking mess. He'd so far managed to keep his guilty secret from Candice, but that would inevitably change and when it did, bang would go his beautiful marriage, to be replaced by certain ruination.

Scott Markham, what have you gone and done?! How many times had he asked himself that question over the past few months? Countless times, that's how many. Thousands, he owed thousands: tens of thousands, more than he could ever hope to pay back on his meagre income. Then he'd met Jonas, through a man who knew a man; Jonas, who had promised to help him settle his debts, at least long enough to give him breathing space, and it had worked, for a while, but Jonas wasn't lending him money out of the goodness of his heart, Christ no, Jonas expected a healthy return for his endeavours. Scott knew that much when he entered into the deal, he wasn't entirely stupid, but he never expected Jonas to push the interest rate up to the level he had. No, he wasn't entirely stupid, just stupidly naive. In the end it was a case of having to rob Peter to pay Paul, to pay Peter to pay Paul and so on and so forth; a vicious circle to be sure. The time was always going to come when the house of cards he'd unwittingly built would come tumbling down to bury him alive—he just never thought it would be so soon.

Jonas had phoned him that morning, not long after he'd waved goodbye to his young wife and daughter-phoned him to call in the debt in its entirety.

"Give me more time," Scott had pleaded into his mobile phone as he'd walked along the pavement to the train station.

"Two days," Jonas had abruptly replied. "You got two days."

"And if I can't pay up?"

"Two days!" The line went dead. Scott had continued his short journey to the train station on weak, shaky legs, feeling very much like a condemned man. It was over, he was finished. He was going to lose his marriage, his home, his career, even—he was an accountant by trade, and everyone knew accountants and bad debts didn't go together. Moreover, he'd heard the rumours surrounding Jonas. The man was ruthless. He showed no mercy, and whilst he employed henchmen to dish out rough justice, he also enjoyed adding the personal touch: tooth and fingernail extraction, knee capping, but there was talk of worse, much worse. So this is to be my fate, Scott had thought fearfully as he stood on the train station platform that fateful morning: personal and financial ruin, or physical torture or both. Not much of a choice, when it came right down to it.

Now, as Scott sat in the tiny office waiting for the man opposite him to begin explaining what the hell was going on around here, he had another stab at trying to work out where he was, but it was useless. Seemed he'd developed a serious case of amnesia—from the stress, probably. His mind was trying to blank things out; a mental safety mechanism. Yeah, that was it. Scott studied the man more closely. He was distinguished, in his mid to late fifties with silver grey hair and intense blue eyes. He wore a dark blue suit, the jacket presently hanging over the back of his chair.

It occurred to Scott that this man might possibly be a doctor, a psychiatrist, maybe, but why would he, Scott, find himself in the company of a shrink? Had he suffered some kind of breakdown, was that it, and been admitted to a psychiatric unit? It might go some way to explaining his confused state of mind, and the apparent amnesia. It was certainly possible: the waiting room he'd just vacated could have been a hospital waiting area, with its white windowless walls and cold sterile atmosphere. There had been a hell of a lot of people in there at any one time: men, women, children, babies—all waiting, but for what? What exactly was this place?

Scott inwardly castigated himself for lacking the presence of mind to make enquiries while he was in there, or at least ask the simple question: "Where the hell am I?" But he hadn't thought to. Why was that, he wondered. The waiting area had given him the creeps. Deathly quiet, it had been. Come to think of it, he failed to recall anyone so much as speaking. Everyone sat perfectly still and waited. Didn't even flick through magazines or read books, just sat there with what could only be described as an air of resignation. It was quite possibly how he himself had come across, now he came to think about it.

A constant stream of people had entered that waiting area whilst he was present, but the numbers never varied, due to the fact that people exited into adjoining rooms in equal measure. In, out, in, out: a constant flow of people passed through. Did they all have the same burning questions on their mind as he did, Scott now wondered as he waited for the man sitting opposite him to put him out of his misery.

After what seemed like an eternity, but which might have been mere seconds, the man finally looked up and introduced himself. "My name is Spires, Mr Markham. My job today is to explain something of extreme importance to you."

Scott cocked an ear. "And what might that be exactly?"

Spires raised a hand. "All in good time. First things first: can I interest you in a drink? Tea, coffee or a soft drink, perhaps?"

"Nothing, thanks," Scott replied, wishing the man would cut to the chase. Glancing around the room, he was struck by the fact that, aside from the desk and two chairs upon which he and Spires sat, the room was completely bare. There was no phone, no computer, no nothing, and there was no intercom, so it couldn't have been Spires who'd called him into the office, like he'd assumed. Now he came to think about it, though, he couldn't actually remember being called into the room by anyone. What the devil goes on? Had somebody simply beamed him up?

"What is this place?" he asked the other man, his confusion and frustration rising.

Spires settled back in his seat, hands folded across his stomach, and said, "We call it The Help Clinic, Mr Markham."

"The Help Clinic," Scott repeated. "And would you mind telling me why I'm here?"

Spires ignored the question and asked his own.

"What is your last memory before entering this establishment?"

Scott found himself having to think hard, very hard. He could remember waving goodbye to Candice, and receiving the phone call from Jonas, and he could remember, albeit vaguely, being in the train station, and then....nothing, zilch.

"I was standing on the station platform waiting for my train," he said whilst struggling to uncover a more recent memory.

Spires nodded thoughtfully: "And then what?"

All of a sudden, Scott broke out in a cold, clammy sweat. He really didn't like that question, but he couldn't put his finger on the reason why. All he knew was he had no wish to remember past the point where he'd been standing on the platform. Why not? Had Jonas appeared at his shoulder brandishing a pair of pliers or a baseball bat? Had he jumped in front of the train? He shuddered at the thought. But that was crazy because if he had, he would be dead, surely, and even if he'd survived a suicide attempt, he'd be in no fit state to be sitting here talking to Spires, or would he?

"Did you actually board the train?" Spires prompted.

Scott wracked his brains, trying to think, but nothing would come.

"I can't remember," he finally admitted.

"It's rare that people can in this situation," Spires said knowingly. "It's the guilt, you see. They find it too hard to face up to, and accept."

Scott frowned. "What are you talking about?"

Spires said; "Let's try it another way: do you recall the train pulling into the station and approaching the platform, Mr Markham?"

Scott considered the question, and then nodded.

"And do you remember what was going through your mind at that time?"

"Jonas," Scott said automatically. "I was thinking about Jonas. My head was full of Jonas."

"Correct," said Spires as if he somehow knew the answer. "And how did the thought of Jonas make you feel?"

"Scared," Scott admitted. "I felt terrified."

"What else?"

"I don't understand."

"Jonas was about to destroy your life, Mr Markham; perhaps destroy you in a very physical sense. And then of course, there was your family to consider: what might he do to your wife and child?"

Scott really didn't like the way the conversation was going. "Don't play games Spires. Out with it—what are you getting at?"

"Denial, Mr Markham—you present a classic case of denial."

"Bullshit!"

"I rest my case."

"You're wrong!"

"Then why can't, or won't you remember?"

"Remember what, for Christ's sake?!"

"Think carefully, Mr Markham: what does the thought of Jonas do to you now?"

Scott contemplated the question. "The thought of him doesn't make me feel anything."

"And why do you suppose that is?"

"I have no idea."

"Then I shall enlighten you. The threat is gone. It is as simple as that."

"I killed him? Are you saying I killed him?"

"Not quite..."

"Are you saying someone else did?"

Spires shook his head, no.

"Stop talking in riddles," Scott said, exasperated. "Just tell me what's going on!"

Spires sighed, as if suddenly very weary. "You have to understand Mr Markham; I can help you to remember, but I am forbidden to remember for you. As I said before, this is a help clinic and help and guide is all that we can do here. Now think: we have established that you were standing on the platform waiting for your train to arrive. Correct?"

"Correct."

"Something happened at that point. Can you recall what it was?"

Scott shut his eyes and concentrated. With some effort he managed to conjure up a mental image of himself standing on the platform, and in doing so, gradually developed a sense of how he'd felt at that time. Yes, he was badly scared; scared for himself and for his family, but he was also angry and desperate and so very ashamed. He'd waited for his train to arrive wanting to kill himself, he recalled all of a sudden. And it would have been so easy. All he had to do was jump in front of the damn thing—it was such a quick, simple and effective solution to a pretty dire situation. But to do that would mean he was abandoning his family, leaving them in peril, and he couldn't do that, no matter how concerned he was for his own wellbeing. And the idea of murdering Jonas was laughable. Even if by some miracle he was able to dispose of Jonas he would always be looking back over his shoulder, fearful of revenge attacks. He opened his eyes and saw that Spires was observing him intently.

"Something on your mind?" he enquired of the man.

"I could ask the same question," Spires returned.

Scott frowned and shut his eyes again. Quite suddenly, in his mind's eye he saw himself leaving the station platform. Where was he going? Certainly not to work. He looked purposeful as he left the station. Outside in the street, it was still sunny, he recalled. Then in the blink of an eye, he was standing outside his house, slipping the key resolutely into the front door lock.

And that was the moment it hit him and he burst into floods of tears.

"Oh my God, what have I done?!" He looked across at Spires like a helpless child, his eyes streaming. "How could I do such a thing? What did I hope to achieve?"

"Who knows what goes on in a person's mind?" Spires responded. "We all of us have our breaking point. You thought you were acting in your family's best interests, I suppose. It was the only way you thought you could protect them."

"Where are they?" Scott managed.

"Safe," said Spires.

"Can I see them?"

"Unfortunately not."

"But I can't live without them. They're my world."

"You should have thought of that before."

"What will happen now? Will it be jail? I deserve it."

Spires shook his head and surprised him by saying, "I hardly think so, Mr Markham. There are no jails where you're going."

"I-I don't understand."

"You don't remember what happened after you had finished with your wife and daughter?"

Scott tried to block the memory, but it came anyway. Candice and Gemma, lost to him forever. Bereft and distraught, he'd turned the knife on himself. The wrists, he'd gone for the wrists; a simple and effective way to end the pain and suffering. But it hadn't quite worked out like that. Instead of finding everlasting peace, he was being confronted by Spires, and a terrible sense of impending doom.

"So, there you have it, Mr Markham," said Spires, "The terrible truth is finally laid bare to you."

"This place," Scott said, trying to collect his thoughts, "Is a half-way house, am I right?"

Spires gave a slight nod of the head. "In a manner of speaking. The Help Clinic helps guide individuals through the transition period. Everyone has to go through it, you know. Your situation is nothing unusual. You will have to pay for your crime, of course, but I doubt that you will be consigned to the dreaded basement area. Misguided though you were, your intentions were good. Having said that, neither will you be elevated to the dizzy heights of the roof garden where your dear ones now reside. No, my feeling is that you will be returned to the scene of the crime, where you can contemplate the error of your ways."

"For how long?" Scott asked, but Spires was already gone, as was the white walled room that was his office. In its place was "the scene of the crime" as Spires had referred to Scott's nice, tidy house. It was here that Scott would begin to contemplate the terrible error of his ways.

THE SUMMER DRESS

It's July and we're in the middle of a heat wave. I'm sitting in the study, the coolest place in the house, keeping myself amused playing around on the laptop, surfing the net and checking my e-mails. The windows are wide open and I can hear the fan whirring noisily in the background. On the desk in front of me, within easy reach, is an ice cold glass of lager. I'm just about to take a sip when I hear the key turn in the front door announcing the return of my darling wife, Cheryl, back from the shops, where she's been hunting for a dress to wear at the barbeque we're hosting tomorrow.

She's been on the case for the past two weeks, and has grown increasingly frustrated at not being able to find what she has in mind. It's got to the point where she's threatening to cancel. Whether she does or not is beside the point. If she doesn't get the right dress it won't be worth going ahead anyway: looking her best is essential. Family members are amongst the guests, therefore everything has to be perfect. Any other time, Cheryl is happy to go with the flow, but when it comes to her family, or more particularly, her mother, nothing short of perfection will do.

So I can't help wondering what kind of mood she's in following another onerous and potentially disastrous trip into the world of retail. My question is answered, at least in part, when she calls up the stairs to me.

"I'm home, Jim! I'm home!"

She sounds happy, which to my mind can only mean one thing: at long last her efforts have paid dividends. *She's finally got the dress!* Perhaps now, life can return to some semblance of normality. I hear her hurry up the stairs. Moments later, she bursts into the study, a raven haired beauty carrying an oversized Next bag, barely able to contain her excitement.

"I got it!" she shrieks joyously, waving the bag like it's a trophy.

I do my level best to share in her enthusiasm.

"That's great; absolutely fantastic!"

"Isn't it just? Give me a second; I'm going to try it on so you can see it!"

"Wonderful; you do that."

She rushes from the room and calm reasserts itself - but not for long. Minutes later, she is back, looking more exuberant than she did before. But I guess she has every right to be, because even I can see that the dress is pretty special. It's a daring strapless affair that fits her slender body like a glove. It also does the most amazing job of showing exactly the right amount of flesh: less would spoil the seductive effect; more would be verging on indecent. But there's a minor problem. When she stands in front of the study's large sunlit window the dress suddenly turns transparent. I feel the need to point this out to her, along with the fact that she doesn't appear to be wearing anything underneath.

"I wondered if you'd notice," she says teasingly. "Don't worry sweetheart; this is for your eyes only. Tomorrow I promise to be more refined. So, what do you think of my new purchase? You've been so busy leering at me, you haven't said whether or not you like it."

"Oh, I like it, all right. Trouble is, so will every other male who sees it, including your dear brother-in-law."

She smiles to herself, I dare say imagining the reaction of her strait-laced elder sister. "What's so wrong with causing a little bit of excitement?" she asks, trying to look as if butter wouldn't melt.

"Why, nothing, other than the fact that the women will absolutely hate you for it!"

She grins mischievously. "I can live with it if you can. By the way, haven't you forgotten something?"

"I don't know, have I?"

"You haven't asked me how much it was."

"How much was it?"

"Too much!"

"In that case, perhaps you should return it."

"You wouldn't make me do that, would you?"

"Depends..."

"On what?"

"On how nice you are to me."

Just then the front doorbell goes.

"Who the devil can that be?" I ask, looking at Cheryl as if she should somehow know.

She gives a little shrug and leaves the room, heading for the stairs.

What happens next is......precisely nothing. There is just an awful, lingering silence.

And then the doorbell sounds again.

I call out: "Cheryl? Hey Cheryl, I thought you were getting the door?"

She doesn't answer. I try again, louder this time, but still there is nothing. So I go to the top of the stairs. "Cheryl, where are you?!" I'm almost yelling now. I wait for a response but the house stays silent. In the end, I'm forced to answer the door myself. Two police officers are standing there. They look like they want to be anywhere but here. They introduce themselves and flash their ID cards. The elder one of the two asks me to confirm my name and then his colleague says, "Mind if we come inside, sir? We would like to talk to you."

I allow them to enter and then call out for Cheryl to join us. The officers glance at each other. In the kitchen they inform me of the problem. The words "accident" and "head on" reverberate through my head like a ricocheting bullet. In an instant I flee from the room and race around the house like a madman, screaming Cheryl's name at the top of my voice. Eventually I return to the kitchen, defeated. The officers are where I left them, sitting in silence at the breakfast table, waiting patiently to escort me to the mortuary.

"She was here," I tell them as calmly as I can. "She wanted to show me the dress, you see."

CLEANING UP

The nagging voice rumbles down the stairs like a mini earthquake.

"Arthur Dicks! Where have you put my purse? You know I always put it on the bedside cabinet, and now it's gone. Where have you put it Arthur, you cretin?"

Arthur Dicks rolls his rheumy eyes heavenward, and gives a despairing shake of the head. He is standing at the kitchen sink, his hands covered in soapsuds. He places a dish on the drainer. He is careful to make the minimum amount of noise. Mabel is sensitive to noise, although this is hard to believe as her voice booms through the house for a second time.

"Arthur! Did you hear me? Arthur!"

He leaves the dishes to soak and scurries over to the foot of the stairs.

"Try your vanity cabinet, dear."

"What?!"

"Your vanity cabinet…"

Mabel appears at the top of the stairs, hands perched on large fleshy hips, her big plump head tilted inquiringly to one side.

"Your vanity cabinet," Arthur says for a third time. "I put it in there because I was afraid it would fall down the side of the bed like last time." And the time before, he thinks but does not say. Mabel is always misplacing things and blaming him.

"Idiot!" she snaps. "Why can't you leave things alone?"

Arthur apologises and gazes up at his domineering wife as a frightened schoolboy might do in the presence of a head teacher. Occasionally, he wonders where the sweet little woman he married all those years ago disappeared to. Somewhere along the way, Mabel changed. Arthur stares with fleeting disbelief, wondering how it could have happened.

"And didn't anyone ever tell you it's rude to stare, Arthur, you pea brain?" says Mabel contemptuously.

Arthur apologises again and returns to the dishes in the kitchen. When he finishes that little job, he retrieves the vacuum cleaner from beneath the stairs and plugs it in. Arthur is a house husband. He has been a house husband since he was made redundant from the car factory two years ago. He has tried to get another job, but no one seems interested. He suspects it has something to do with his age. He's one of the over-fifties. It seems to him that once you join that particular club, you become invisible to employers. Mabel has little sympathy for his plight, accusing him of being bone idle, fit for the scrap heap, a waste of time and space, dead meat. She has a way with words, does Mabel.

He switches the vacuum cleaner on. Nothing happens. He rolls his eyes and mumbles under his breath.

"Bugger…"

"What was that?" Mabel is standing behind him.

Arthur flinches and tries to explain: "Vacuum is broken…"

Mabel scowls. "Well, get it fixed, dumbo!"

"Yes, dear."

She squeezes past him, tut-tutting as she goes. Arthur stares impassively, whilst thinking how enormous she is becoming. Weight Watchers doesn't seem to be working for her. In fact, she has ballooned even more since joining up. Arthur is convinced that one day she will simply go pop and be no more. Happy thoughts...

He looks at the vacuum cleaner. Mabel's cat, Smudge, is standing by it. Smudge is a mean-tempered tabby that likes to bring presents in from the garden. Last week, Arthur was surprised to find a dead mouse under the kitchen table. Just before Christmas, it was a bird, minus the head. Occasionally Smudge surpassed himself, bringing giant slugs or spiders into the house. He even brought a dead baby rabbit home once. Arthur had got the blame for that, too. Mabel never tired of attributing blame to others, especially to her dear, beloved husband.

Smudge is staring at him in the only way Smudge can: with sheer loathing.

"Shoo!" says Arthur, and the cat darts off into the kitchen.

"I'm going now, Arthur. Do you hear me?" Mabel is standing by the front door wearing what Arthur refers to as her shopping outfit. She's going into town with her friend, Irene, to buy things. She and Irene are always buying things with which to clutter up their respective homes.

"I said I'm off now," Mabel repeats for Arthur's benefit.

He nods obediently. "Yes, dear."

"I'll be back about five."

Arthur suppresses a strong urge to smile. With Mabel out of the house for the whole of the afternoon, he'll be able to listen to the radio in peace; a rare occurrence indeed.

"What's for dinner?" she barks suddenly, pulling him rudely back to the present.

"Beans on toast," he replies, saying the first thing that pops into his head.

Mabel pulls a face. "Can't you think of anything more adventurous than beans on toast? We had that yesterday!"

"How about a nice 'am omelette?"

"My God, Arthur, you really are beyond hope," says Mabel as a parting gesture, just before she slams the front door shut.

"Love you, too," Arthur mutters with a dejected sigh.

He trots into the lounge and peers through the window, and watches Mabel waddle down the path to the bus stop. Satisfied she won't be returning until the appointed hour, he turns on the radio and tunes it in to Radio 4, his favourite station. Mabel doesn't allow him to have it on when she is home, claiming it is for boring old buggers with nothing better to do. Mabel prefers Radio 2. Arthur returns to the hall, where he inspects the troublesome vacuum cleaner and makes another attempt to get it going. It doesn't respond. He decides the only course of action is to take it to Mr. Ying, who has a little electrical repair shop on the corner of the street. Arthur has never been there before, but he has heard good things about Mr. Ying and the service he provides.

So Arthur puts on his overcoat, deposits the vacuum cleaner in a black bin liner, and then carries it the relatively short distance to Mr. Ying's place. Mr. Ying is working at the back of the shop when he enters. There is a bell on the counter, which Arthur rings. Mr. Ying, who is thin and reedy with sharp eyes and a straggly beard, breaks off from what he is doing, and Arthur explains the problem. Mr. Ying nods and smiles politely, and then takes the vacuum cleaner away with him, returning minutes later, claiming it is fixed.

"Champion" says Arthur, as he pays the modest bill.

"You having big c-rean up?" Mr. Ying asks, nodding and smiling.

"The usual," Arthur replies.

"It's good to get lid of things. You can see wood for t-lees then. And reed a happy rife."

"Most definitely," says Arthur, not really sure he understands.

Back home, Arthur gets straight down to business. The vacuum is amazing. It has never performed better, and Arthur has never enjoyed vacuuming so much. As he swings the suction pad to and fro across the carpet, Smudge happens to wander into the room. Arthur thinks it would be fun to give the cat a little scare and aims the powerful suction pad directly at it. There follows a loud, resonating "whoosh", which sees Smudge suddenly airborne with his fur standing on end, yowling for all he is worth. A moment later, he is nowhere to be seen!

In a blind panic, Arthur switches off the machine and checks the dust bag, but Smudge isn't there: there's only powdery grey dust. Arthur scratches his bald pate in wonderment and for the next half hour searches the house for the missing cat. But why should he worry, he suddenly asks himself. He hated the damn animal. It was Mabel's idea to have it. It's no loss to him. My Ying's words echo through his head all of a sudden.

"It's good to get lid of things. You can see wood for t-lees then. And reed a happy rife."

Most definitely, thinks Arthur with a thoughtful little smile. Having successfully reassembled the vacuum cleaner, he makes himself a cup of tea and retires to the living room, where he listens contentedly to Radio 4.

When Mabel returns home that afternoon, Arthur greets her from behind the door, brandishing the vacuum cleaner's screaming suction pad. Mabel's oversized head goes in much the same way Smudge did hours earlier, followed by her oversized body, which, it has to be said, doesn't go with quite the same ease. In fact, the machine struggles to digest her at first, but then, like some bizarre mechanical boa constrictor, the process is eventually completed with minimal fuss. When Arthur checks the vacuum cleaner's collection bag, there is only thick grey dust, a bit like cremation dust, he thinks, as he empties it into the bin outside.

"It's good to get lid of things," he says to himself as he ambles back inside the house, crying tears of laughter. "You can see wood for t-lees then, and reed a happy rife!"

MAN'S BEST FRIEND

I hit the dog at over forty miles per hour. It was an albino boxer and it didn't stand a chance. I heard the thud, saw the mutt hit the side of the road and made the split second decision to keep on going. It was late, and no one was about—I counted myself lucky, I'd been drinking and didn't need the cops around me, which is what might have happened had I done the right thing, and stopped to see if the dog was okay.

By the time I arrived home, Maggie was asleep in bed. I was relieved. It meant I didn't have to explain my lateness or the smell of alcohol on my breath. I elected to sleep in the spare room that night, so as not to disturb her.

In the morning, all was well with the world. Sure, Maggie grilled me as to where I'd been all night, and why I hadn't phoned to let her know I was going to be late or kept my mobile phone on. She even scolded me for my inconsideration, albeit in a rudimentary fashion (she didn't really have much of a temper), but then melted when I flashed my winning smile and promised to make amends.

My excuse for being late—I was entertaining an important client. The client was, in fact, a good-time girl called Angie. We'd met at a bar while Maggie was away staying at her mum's; kind of hit it off, then had it off, and continued to do so at every given opportunity. She was everything Maggie wasn't: lewd, crude and rude, and when it came to the bedroom, she went like a Duracell rabbit. I was one happy guy: a faithful, loving wife at home, and a whore with whom to amuse myself on away days.

So Maggie accepted my story and forgave me just like she always did, and fell straight back into the role of the trusting little wife. "Naiveté" was her middle name. When we first met, I thought that with her it was a case of still waters run deep, when in actual fact it was more like, what you see is what you get: I don't mean to be cruel, but the phrase "nice but dim" springs to mind. To her credit, Maggie was kind hearted, dependable, and most importantly to me, she had an understanding nature. And I needed a lot of that: I tended to drink far more than was good for me, and as you may have already gathered, I had a keen eye for the ladies.

The dog was gone when I drove past the accident spot on the way to work the following morning, which meant either its body had been taken away in a council van already, or it'd survived and managed to walk away, which in my estimation was a total impossibility. I'd hit the mutt with the force of a speeding train!

The damage to the front bumper was minimal. Unfortunately, Maggie clocked it and asked how it happened.

"It was done in the restaurant car park while I was dining with my client," I lied. "Bastard didn't even have the courtesy to leave a card or phone number, sugar pops."

The insurance company agreed to pay for the repair, minus the excess, which meant the matter could be put to bed without any fuss. Seemed I'd had a lucky escape. Life carried on as normal.

Until, that is, the dog turned up on my doorstep one afternoon while Maggie was out shopping. It was in the back garden sitting on the patio, looking as large as life and twice as dippy, gazing dumbly through the patio window, slavering like something rabid. I banged on the glass and shouted for it to "get!" It remained sitting there unflinchingly, staring up at me through mournful brown eyes.

"Get! Shoo! Bugger off, Fido!"

It simply stared. And then it raised a paw that seemed to say, "Shake; let's make friends," or maybe, I thought suddenly, it was metaphorically pointing the finger, signalling its intention to get even.

Blood covered the side of its head just below one ear. The sight of it caused a huge pang of guilt to shoot through me. To experience guilt was a new concept for me, and I didn't like it one little bit. To hell with this, I thought, this was no time for sentiment, it was a time for action, the dog had no right to be here and it needed to be gotten rid of. I banged on the glass again, angrily, but to no effect. The dumb mutt continued to stare up at me through dark, imploring eyes. When that failed to gain my sympathy, it whimpered like a frightened pup.

"How'd you survive?" I asked it through the glass. More importantly I thought uneasily, how'd you find out where I live; how did you, a dumbass animal, manage to track me down when I live miles from where the accident happened?

It offered no answer, of course, but continued to gaze up at me with its annoying hang-dog expression and its stupid paw raised pathetically in mid-air. I banged on the glass again, this time so hard it shook in its frame, but the dog didn't even flinch. It just sat there; paw elevated, tongue lolling, eyeing me like I was its long lost-friend and master.

The sound of a key being inserted into the front door lock got my attention. Maggie was back. As if on cue, the dog rose, somewhat stiffly, turned and then walked off across the patio towards the garden, only it didn't walk in the true sense of the word, it kind of lurched and staggered as if drunk. But then it had taken a hit that would have flattened a full-grown elephant, I reminded myself.

Maggie's girly voice drifted irritatingly through the house. "Kieran, I'm home, hon!"

I opened my mouth to answer but the sight of the dog's weird gait rendered me speechless. The thing actually collapsed at one point: simply fell down, like a puppet whose strings have been cut. Then it was up on all fours again, a shambling canine wreck, heading towards the gate at the bottom of the garden, which incidentally, was wide open, when I distinctly remembered closing it following my morning jog. I made it a habit to check that it was properly closed as it led directly into a field where sheep grazed. After dark or whenever Maggie and I were both out of the house, I padlocked that gate, so I was careful, and I knew it'd been closed.

I watched the dog progress unsteadily to the bottom of the garden and through the gate, where it slowly turned and disappeared from view, and then, having had to make a conscious effort to compose myself, I went to greet Maggie.

She could sense something had unsettled me—she might have been dim but she wasn't stupid—and asked me what was wrong.

"Nothing," I said a little more defensively than I intended.

"Are you sure, babe?"

"Of course."

"Only you look a bit pale."

"I'm fine, sugar pops: honest."

In bed that night, I was woken by a dog's insistent barking. It came from outside in the back garden. I crept out of bed and stole myself to peep through the curtains that overlooked the patio area.

And there sat the blasted dog, pale and ghostly beneath an incandescent moon, gazing up at me with the same doleful expression as before. I checked to make sure Maggie hadn't woken, slipped on my dressing gown and made my way quietly downstairs into the kitchen where I grabbed the torch from under the sink, before unlocking and opening the back door. With the torch switched on, I took the path that led to the patio, having first collected the gardening fork from the shed.

We stood facing each other, neither of us moving for the longest time. I had no idea what my game plan was. I simply wanted rid. I took a tentative step forwards. The dog stood, awkwardly, its whole body quivering, as if the action caused it distress. Plainly, it was injured. I had the upper hand, it seemed. I've always been a go getter, an "in for the kill" kind of guy, so I did what came naturally: I instinctively went on the attack, lunging with the gardening fork in the hope the dog would flee, but amazingly, it failed to move or even make a sound, forcing me to stop dead in my tracks, and rethink my plan of action.

The word "stalemate" sprang to mind.

Then the ruddy animal raised its paw just like it had before, in a kind of "let's be friends" gesture.

"Get!" I snarled, but it stubbornly refused. "Go on, get!"

Directly above me, a window opened and a puzzled-sounding voice said, "Kieran, what on earth are you doing down there?"

I glanced up to find Maggie staring down at me. "This bloody dog," I tried to explain, "was barking its stupid head off right outside our bedroom window!"

"What dog?" Maggie asked, peering around curiously.

"This dog," I said pointing, but when I looked the dog was gone.

Then Maggie was speaking again, urging me to return to bed.

So that's what I did, but not before I took one last look round, and in the process spotted the dark pool of blood where the dog had been.

xx

"I'm sorry Angie, but I can't meet you tonight. Maggie has changed her mind about going away and expects me to take her out to dinner."

"That's bollocks, Kieran, and you know it," Angie snapped back. "You just don't want to see me."

Before I could answer, the line went dead. I was parked up on the roadside shaking like crazy, unable to function, not because of Angie's call, but because I'd just avoided hitting the dog again. It'd appeared out of nowhere, forcing me to swerve into oncoming traffic in an attempt to avoid it. Having narrowly escaped a head-on collision with an articulated lorry, I'd come to a sudden halt on the hard shoulder, at which point Angie had called my mobile.

I thought about what she'd said and called her back.

"Angie, listen to me. It's not that I don't want to see you; of course I do, but it can be difficult at times."

"Don't fuck with me Kieran, or your better half might suddenly find out about how the two of us spend our time together!"

With that, the line went dead again.

I shook like a leaf all the way home. I was in a bad way. I felt like my life was spiralling out of control: my concentration was suffering: work was suffering. I could hardly sleep, and when I did, I dreamed about the damn dog. I was turning to the bottle more and more as a source of comfort.

Things escalated when the dog tracked me down to my place of work. One afternoon upon leaving the office, I found it waiting for me; sitting by my car, staring morosely. It was too much for me to take. I completely lost it, ranted and raved, kicked out, catching the animal along its flank. It yelped pitifully and staggered off between two rows of parked cars before disappearing round a corner.

A parking attendant appeared on the scene at that point, and asked me what the problem was. I tried to explain about the dog. He gave me a funny look, shook his head and wandered off. I got in my car. First thing I did was grab the vodka bottle I'd taken to keeping in the glove compartment. I needed something to calm my nerves.

That night, the dog turned up again. I knew it would; it was intent on stalking me. Payback for the pain and distress I'd put it through. This time, I was ready for it.

As it passed through the gate at the bottom of the garden, which I'd purposely left open, I took an axe to its head, striking it repeatedly until it collapsed in an unmoving bloody heap. Then, shaking from the adrenalin rush, I dragged its lifeless body over to the hole I'd dug in readiness, and buried it there, in the hope that life would finally return to normal.

But that didn't happen. Next morning, I found the grave open with the dog nowhere to be seen. All I could do was wait and see what other nasty surprises were in store for me. In the meantime there was Angie to contend with. She was demanding more and more of my time and growing increasingly frustrated when I failed to meet with her demands. But how could I; the situation with the dog was driving me crazy! In the end, Angie went through with her threat to tell Maggie about our affair.

"How could you?" Maggie blurted tearfully when she found out.

"I'm sorry, sugar pops. Truly I am."

"Is that all you have to say for yourself?"

When I tried to give her a comforting hug, she slapped my face and told me to pack my bags and leave. It seemed that the mouse, or "mouse wife", as I fondly thought of her, had finally found the courage to roar!

As a result, I was forced to get a place of my own—a cheap, dingy maisonette in a less than desirable location. I could afford little else after losing my job. It was the dog's fault - damn thing ran out into the road, causing me to crash the car. I'd been at the vodka bottle again and failed the breathalyser test. My company had no other option but to release me from my contract.

But hey, let's be positive. I did have a home, such as it was, and I had company, of a type, in the form of the dog. Damn thing was there on the day I moved in, waiting patiently for me outside the front entrance, its head a gory mess, its short white fur caked in blood and soil. Pretty it was not, but at least it wanted to know me when no one else did. So I took it in, stitched its broken skull as best I could, cleaned it up so it looked and smelled better, and made a promise to never, ever abuse it again. It was, I thought, the least I could do.

THE ETERNAL TRIANGLE

When he enters the kitchen, she is standing with her back to him gazing out of the window.

"Hello, Annie," he says, by way of greeting. "It's good to see you again."

"Is it?" she asks, turning to face him, "is it really, Pete?"

"Don't be like that, Annie. I always look forward to your visits."

"And yet you look so forlorn..."

"I find it difficult to deal with my emotions because of what happened, Annie, but it doesn't mean I don't like to see you. I mean to say, we've had some fantastic times together, you and I; fun times. Remember when we visited America; New York, for Christmas shopping. Only two days, a flying visit, but what fun we had."

She nods and smiles. "Yes, Pete, I remember. It was wonderful."

"I love you, Annie, always have; always will."

"I know you do," she says softly. And then she returns her attention to the outside view and the moment is gone. Pete watches, captivated as her pony-tail, tied by a slender red ribbon, gently sways with the subtle movement of her head. He watches enthralled, happy to have her back again. He takes a seat at the kitchen table just as Jean walks in.

"I heard you talking," she tells him whilst ignoring the other woman.

"Annie and I were reminiscing," he replies.

"I thought as much," she says, joining him at the table. He suddenly finds himself studying Jean's face as if for the first time: the lines that reflect her advanced years, the dull quality affecting her once vibrant green eyes, the crow's feet now framing them; and her hair, the grey roots, peeping through the dark unflattering rinse she insists on using. She looks tired, he thinks to himself, worn down by so many years that have passed never to be recaptured. Her youth is gone forever. Just like mine, he muses. Yet he can't help yearning for what is lost and can never be regained.

"Are you all right, Pete?"

Her words pull him back to the present and he manages a faint smile for her benefit.

"You looked so sad just then," she says in almost a whisper. "Is it because Annie's here, or is it me Pete? Do I make you feel sad?"

He ignores the question and looks over at Annie, who is now standing by the French doors, gazing out across the back garden to the patio area beyond, upon which stands an ornate summerhouse.

"The garden looks lovely this time of year," he says wistfully.

"Never better," Jean agrees.

Annie turns and smiles at him. The smile melts his heart. He continues to stare, his expression full of yearning and regret.

Jean sighs resignedly. "Are you happy with me, Pete?"

"You know I am," he says, reaching for her hand.

Then Annie speaks, "Will you be here when I visit next year, Pete?"

He nods and smiles at her. "Of course; how could I possibly leave?"

"How indeed..."

"You could always stay this time," he suggests, but Annie shakes her head. "You know I can't do that."

"Then at least say you forgive me."

"I can't."

"Pete, you're upsetting yourself," Jean says intuitively, but he ignores her.

"You can't possibly imagine what it's like," he tells Annie, oblivious to Jean's feelings. "Every time I see you I'm reminded of just how much I lost—how much we both lost."

"That's why I visit," says Annie, "To remind you."

"You're being unfair."

"You reap what you sow, Pete."

Lost for words, Pete returns his attention to the French doors and the garden beyond.

"Are you all right?" It's Jean.

"I'm fine," he tells her.

"You don't look it."

"Really, I'm fine."

He tries to smile but this time, fails.

"Poor Pete," says Jean.

"You mustn't feel sorry for me," he tells her, and then Annie speaks. "I don't feel sorry for you, Pete, not in the slightest."

He regards the two women in silence and can't help making comparisons. They are complete opposites, he thinks, Jean being steadfast and loyal, while Annie is impulsive and unpredictable. And yet, he loves them both in equal measure.

And then Jean is withdrawing her hand from his and rises slowly from her seat.

"Back to normal tomorrow, eh, Pete?" she says forcing a smile.

Pete acknowledges the statement with a vague nod of the head, whilst gazing intently at Annie. All these years, he thinks but does not say. All these years dead, and yet you refuse to leave me completely, returning every year to mark the anniversary of our parting.

"Tell me something," Jean says, bringing him back to the present once more. "And do please be honest, Pete. All things being equal; who would you choose? Which of us would you rather be with?"

"You," he says unhesitatingly.

"It's kind of you to say that."

"I mean it, Jean. Unlike Annie, you've stayed faithful to me."

"So what became of her?" Jean asks, following a brief silence. "You never did tell me."

Pete answers the question with a sigh. And then, as if to himself: "Had she remained loyal, doubtless things would have been different and she'd still be here today."

"And we wouldn't be together," Jean points out.

But Pete isn't listening, for he is observing Annie as she returns to her final resting place beneath the patio, upon which the summerhouse stands.

COLD COMFORT

I was always an anxious child. I don't know why, but I worried about everything: losing things, what people thought of me, did they like me or hate me? Mum was always telling me I would worry myself into an early grave. "Pity your husband," she'd say, "you'll worry him to certain death with all your worrying!" Even Dad had the odd go at me. "Honestly Jane, you would worry yourself silly even if you had nothing to worry about!"

When I got older I overheard mum tell my Nan I was paranoid, and I worried myself about that too. I looked the word up in the dictionary and was horrified to discover that being paranoid is to be suspicious, fearful, mistrustful, obsessed and unreasonable. I was horrified because I could see how those words related to me. I was, and still am all of those things. I didn't even trust my own parents or my elder sister, Mary. Mary used to say I was scared of my own shadow and would put me down in front of people. Mary was the ambitious, pretty one, and boy did she let me know it. "Plain Jane" was her pet expression for me. Or "mouse". "Want some cheese, mouse?" What's wrong, mouse, cat got your tongue?" And she would laugh until she cried. She thought it was hilarious. What, with Mary saying things like that, and mum saying I was paranoid, I would end up worrying myself half crazy!

The kids at school didn't really help. I think they thought I was a bit strange. I didn't talk much and kept myself to myself. I ended up with the nickname, "Worry Wart". It's not really surprising I developed a bit of a complex. I withdrew into myself more and more. I found it impossible to articulate my thoughts and feelings, other than by recording them on paper. But that would only make me more frustrated. In the end I simply gave up trying to relate to people, and refused to communicate with anyone, my parents; Mary, even the doctors that my despairing parents sent me to. This period of my life dogged me into my teenage years.

During this anxiety ridden time I was tutored at home by Mum, which was ridiculous. She was semi literate, with the patience of a bear with a sore head. I learnt absolutely nothing and ended up as ill educated as her. But what could Mum or anyone else do? I simply refused to co-operate. Dealing with me must have been a nightmare. When I think about it, I don't know how they put up with me. I'm surprised they didn't have me locked away. Maybe they tried. It's something I'll never know. When I was thirteen, Mum, Dad and Mary were killed in a road accident. Suddenly I was an orphan. I always worried that something bad would happen to my family. I always felt that I was a bit of a walking disaster; that I would heap bad luck upon anyone who came into contact with me. I guess I'm what you could call a self fulfilling prophecy.

I was adopted by a decent, hard working couple, the Smiths - Eric and Margaret. They were an older, childless couple. I took their name and became Jane Smith: "plain Jane Smith," I could imagine my late sister saying, "How very apt," and she would have laughed hysterically. Eric and Marge, as Margaret was known, heaped a huge amount of love and affection on me. Gradually, I started to come out of my shell. I grew in confidence and returned to full time education. Even though I appeared happier and more self assured, underneath the surface I was as insecure as ever, and continued to worry about everything. Despite my good fortune in finding the Smiths to fill the void left by the death of my parents, I was still a tormented soul. I simply hid it better. Amongst other things, I worried that my new mum and dad would go the same way as my real parents, and die prematurely.

And guess what—it happened. When I was twenty, they suddenly died within weeks of one another. Eric got run over by a bus. He refused to use the underpass saying it was dangerous—such irony! And then Marge died of a heart attack. Everyone said it was probably the shock of Eric's death. I started to think of myself as a "Jonah". The Smiths left me every last penny they had, which was not an inconsiderable amount. I guess I was quite eligible despite my plain looks and introverted personality. After all, not many twenty year olds can lay claim to having their own mortgage-free home, a nice car in the drive, and a tidy sum in the bank. Yet, still I worried myself senseless. I worried about my future, about the fact I was alone and friendless. I even worried about dying alone. I was twenty for God's sake, and I was thinking about dying alone in old age!

I continued to worry myself over almost anything: from doing the shopping and maintaining the house, to the state of the world economy. I worried about the little kids starving to death in third world countries and started giving money. I worried about the elderly, and how they managed, and gave to charities like Help the Aged. Then I started to worry about people dying of cancer, and gave to the Macmillan Cancer fund. Then I worried that I might get cancer myself, and very nearly made myself ill through all the worry.

Recognising I was on a downward spiral, I visited my GP, who prescribed pills for my condition, but they made me worse, so I stopped taking them. I became increasingly withdrawn, ending up a virtual recluse.

By now, I'd left full-time education, was unemployed and spent most days sitting around the house trying to control my anxiety. I had no friends and no existing relatives. I knew I must do something radical to get myself out of the rut I was in, and so I did. I pulled myself together—or at least, as together as I could get, given the fact I was scared to death of life itself—got some private counselling and joined a writing group. As I said, I've always written, recording my thoughts and feelings mainly, which, as you can see from this example, doesn't make particularly uplifting reading.

So I joined a writing group, and guess what? A minor miracle occurred. I found myself adopted by another family, only this time I had something in common with its members. Writing! Not only that, I met a man called Simon, who seemed to like me. We clicked and would talk endlessly about anything under the sun. Even my anxiety! Simon seemed to understand where I was coming from. More than that, he empathised. Empathy was something I'd never experienced before.

We started to date. Simon was my first ever boyfriend and I worried that I'd be unable to cope with, well, the worry of having a partner, someone I truly cared for. But I needn't have concerned myself, as it turned out. He did all the worrying for me—well, almost all. Eventually, he moved in with me. Six months later, we got engaged. The following summer, we married. Not long after that, Harry arrived, followed by Becky.

For a time I was happy, and my anxiety became less of a problem. I still worried about every little thing, but my life had purpose and direction now. I was busy looking after my own family, and the distraction helped me to forget my irrational worries. Until night came, that is. I would lie awake worrying about Simon and the kids. What if something happened to them—say they got killed, like my parents, my sister, and my adoptive parents? Life could be cruel; I knew that much from personal experience. There were no guarantees. Events could turn just like that! One moment you could be as happy as Larry, whoever Larry was - the next, catastrophe!

And guess what—that's exactly what happened! Simon met someone else and left me. Just like that. "Jane, I've met someone. I'll be moving out. I'm sorry, but it's not working. It'll be better for both of us. Trust me." Trust him! The irony of those words! So he moved out and went to live with his mistress and the koala bears in sunny Australia, leaving me with the responsibility of the kids. Not only that, but he'd somehow managed to mortgage the house behind my back, which threatened to leave us destitute. It all got on top of me in the end. I'd always been a bit of a collector, ornamental pigs, teapots, plates and dishes, soft furnishings, whatever takes my fancy. My collecting suddenly escalated. I ended up hoarding anything and everything. In no time, the house was filled to the rafters with clutter.

If that wasn't bad enough, I developed an eating disorder, convincing myself that frozen meals were the only safe source of food. As a result, I purchased a sizeable chest freezer to go with my more modest fridge freezer, which I then filled to the brim with frozen meals. I was a complete mess, I knew it, but was unable to do anything about it. In an attempt to distract myself from my woes, and cheer up the kids, I got us a little pet hamster that we named, Hammy—what else? In the months that followed, Hammy became a part of the family.

But then, just like my parents and my sister, and my adoptive parents, death stole him away. Unable to tell Harry and Becky the sad truth, I said he'd escaped and run off. In reality he remained far closer to home, buried beneath the ice and frozen food packages, at the bottom of the chest freezer. I simply couldn't bring myself to part with him.

Hammy's death only served to increase my concern for Harry and Becky's well being, especially their safety. I refused to allow them out to play with other kids after school, worried they might be abducted by one of the freaks you read about. And the roads—the roads are death traps nowadays. Too much traffic! I drove them everywhere. I had to. I was a single mum and it was my job to protect the little mites. At the slightest sign of a cold I would rush them to the doctor; afraid they would develop pneumonia and die. I was haunted by the spectre of Death, it seemed. Nobody ever stayed with me. All those close to me ended up leaving. I was so scared that Harry and Becky would be taken away from me too. There are so many dangers to consider these days, I thought. Paedophiles seem to be lurking on every street corner. Hoodies roam the streets in packs stabbing people if they so much as get looked at. You're not even safe in your own home!

I had to think of a way to protect myself and my children from the horrors of life, I decided. As a consequence, I suffered endless sleepless nights. And then, one day my worst fears were realised. I received a phone call from a social worker. The school or someone at the school had reported me for neglecting Harry and Becky, and keeping them away from lessons. It was the final straw. I lay in bed that night completely traumatised. It appeared that my lifelong suspicions had been proved right. Nobody could be trusted in this world. They either left you, or they betrayed you.

In the days and nights that followed, I continued to worry constantly that Harry and Becky would be ripped from my life, just like everyone else I'd ever loved. I tortured myself over what to do for the best. I couldn't stand the thought of my two little sweethearts being taken from me, but I was also forced to accept that I was no longer able to cope with the constant anxiety of looking after them. In the end, after much deliberation, I reached a decision.

I'm afraid it's all a bit of a blur after that. What I do recall quite clearly, however, is the feeling of sheer panic I experienced when the electricity was cut off following my failure to pay the bill, and the horrendous surge of dread that followed when the bailiffs arrived on the doorstep with an eviction order.

And I recall also, with crystal clarity, the look of abject horror and revulsion that filled the faces of those people when the stench inside the house hit him, and they discovered the whereabouts of Hammy, Harry and Becky.

COMING OF AGE

I am lost in a game of Patience when unexpectedly my father summons me to his study to tell me a tale. This surprises me as he has never told me a story before, and I go eagerly.

I settle down, cross-legged on the floor while he occupies the big leather chair over by his desk. Nearby, a fire blazes in the grate. Through the study window, I watch snow drift from the clear night sky, while high above the forest next to our house hangs a dazzling full moon.

"What kind of story is it?" I ask. I am excited to have my father's undivided attention and expectant as to the nature of the story I am to hear.

He clasps his big, strong hands together in his lap and smiles. He reminds me of a bear with his thick dark hair and great bushy beard—or a wolf, perhaps? He is a man in his middle years, is my father: a big man, as tall and as broad as a mountain in my young eyes. Mother says he looks good for his age and that I will grow up to be just like him. As for myself, I have just turned twelve, although I have heard it said that I have an "old head on young shoulders". My mother also says that being twelve is a milestone, but doesn't say why. It would be nice, I think, to discover the secret before I am thirteen.

Father breaks the silence by saying, "The story I am about to tell is a dark one, son, but you must not be afraid."

"Dark as in scary?" I ask.

"No," he says, "Dark. There's a difference."

He smiles at my obvious confusion. At least I think it's a smile. It's hard to tell, for the lighting in the study is low, and his features are distorted by shadow.

And so, he begins to tell the tale of how a boy, who is a special boy and doesn't yet know it, comes of age. It is a startling change, he says. He uses the word "metamorphosis", and has to explain its meaning. He says the boy is special because he is different.

"In much the same way you are," he adds thoughtfully.

"But I don't want to be different," I quickly reply. "I want to be the same as everyone else."

To this he nods his head and sighs. "Sometimes, son, things happen that don't appear to make much sense at first. Life can seem unfair, but there's always a reason for what happens, if you look hard enough."

I get the feeling he is trying to tell me something that I may not like.

"You mustn't look so concerned," he says as if reading my mind.

But I am, and I reply, "First you say you are telling me a dark story. Now you're saying that life is unfair. I wonder if you are trying to prepare me for bad news."

He smiles. His teeth shine whitely through his beard. His eyes glint sharply in the reflected light of the fire. Momentarily, they remind me of a wolf's eyes. Although I know this must be an illusion, they hold me spellbound. After what seems like a long time I am able to look away.

Through the window I spy the silvery moon. It is perfectly round and gloriously bright, and draws my mind away from reality. All at once, I feel different. My body is no longer my own. It is as if it is changing into something else.

I am afraid to look. I close my eyes as if to shut out the truth and start to drift, but then my father speaks again, urging me to pay attention. I snap my eyes open and sit up straight.

He nods his head, pacified, and then continues with his tale. "When finally the boy came of age, he stood proud and fearless, a formidable creature of the night whose enemies were few, and whose life would be long and fulfilled."

I begin to smile, liking what I hear, until that is, father leans forward and frowns. All of a sudden I'm thinking, here it is; the bad news I sensed would come: the one single detail that will make this a "dark" story.

Raising a cautionary finger that more resembles a claw, father says in a low gruff voice, "Take heed, my son, this very special child is by no means invincible, and must respect his enemies and beware the danger they represent."

That said, father turns his head towards the window so he is in profile. I am astounded to see that his nose has taken on the characteristics of a long pointed snout. Suddenly, a dark resonating growl rises from deep within his throat. When he looks at me again, he is no longer the father I know. Before I can fully comprehend what has happened, my mother emerges from the hallway. She too is different—changed—as I myself am. Metamorphosed, my father would no doubt say. This is the darkness he spoke of in the story—the darkness that is manifest in my family.

I turn to him. He instructs me to go forth into the woods with my mother while he guards the family home.

"Learn from her endeavours," he advises in a voice that rumbles like thunder. I nod my head obediently, rise and pad quickly across the room to join her. She is already making her way to the back of the house, and to the big, dark wood that lies beyond.

I feel empowered. Outside moonshine lights our way. I pause at the gate at the bottom of our garden. I can hear my mother's voice whispering to me inside my head. "*Twelve is a special age,*" she is saying, "*You, my son, are a special boy.*" A long, mournful howl then fills the night air, and suddenly I glimpse sight of her in the distance. Her head is raised heavenwards towards the glittering moon. She howls once more, longingly, and is answered by others of our kind. I imitate her poorly, but will improve, I am sure.

The wood awaits us, as does our quarry. I sniff the air for a scent and I growl fiercely, or as fiercely as I am able. Tonight I will race the moon, hunt with the pack and be in at the kill. My mother, the she-wolf, reads my mind. She seems pleased with me. As she slinks off into the darkness, I follow, knowing that I am about to come of age.

THE UNINVITED

Tim Christopher first became aware of the old woman shortly after taking up residence at the "The Birches". He was busy loading rubbish into a skip on his driveway when he saw her leaving the nature reserve across the road. She was thin and sour faced and walked with the aid of a cane. She came to stand on the pavement where she paused to look directly at the house.

"Nice day," Tim called out to her. The woman ignored him. He tried again. Same result. "Love you too, you old misery," he said beneath his breath.

"Who are you talking to?" asked a voice from behind.

He turned to see his wife standing there.

"The old dear," he said.

"What old dear?"

He looked back across the road. The woman was gone.

"You were talking to yourself again, weren't you," Helen Christopher teased. "You do realise it's the first sign of madness."

"I'll mention it to my psychiatrist," Tim countered. "By the way, have you seen our wayward son lately?"

"Last time I saw Adam he was in the back garden," Helen said. "Why do you ask?"

Tim pointed to the bicycle lying on the pavement. "Blessed thing's going to get stolen if he's not more careful."

Inside the house Helen poured Tim a glass of tap water. "Drink," she said, "or you'll get dehydrated."

Tim did as he was told. "I tell you, Helen, the gardens surrounding this house are a jungle. They'll be the death of me, I swear."

Helen, putting dishes away in one of the cupboards, said, "You can't die just yet; you've got wallpaper stripping next."

"Thanks for the sympathy," Tim replied as he wandered into the utility room to wash his hands.

"You wanted to buy the place," Helen pointed out, following with a basket of laundry.

"We both did," Tim reminded her.

They had offered on "The Birches" in March of that year, before finally completing and moving in at the beginning of August. The sale had been protracted due to survey problems, which had resulted in re-negotiation; a situation further complicated by the fact that the owner refused to have any direct involvement in the sale, preferring instead to employ the services of a relative.

"The Birches" was ramshackle, but habitable, with immense potential, a fact not lost on the Christophers. The couple saw it as more than an investment however; they intended it to be their forever home. Perched on a large corner plot with original features intact, it overlooked a sprawling nature reserve. It was, the Christophers thought, the perfect place in which they and their seven year old son could grow and prosper.

"How're you doing with the unpacking?" Tim asked Helen as he dried his hands.

"Getting there, slowly," she replied.

"Slowly, slowly catchy monkey," Tim said, playfully grabbing her from behind.

The sound of a creaking door distracted them. They turned to see Adam standing in the doorway.

"Hey, what's up soldier?" Tim asked.

The boy, who was fair skinned and fair haired like his parents, and small for his age, looked vaguely troubled. Pointing back the way he'd come, he said, "There's a lady in the garden."

"A lady," Tim repeated, "What does she want?"

"She asked me if she could come into the house."

Tim exchanged a puzzled look with Helen.

"What did you say?"

"I told her I'd ask you."

"You did the right thing," Tim said. "Where's the lady now?"

"Not sure."

"What did she look like?" asked Helen.

"Old" said Adam, "with a walking stick."

Tim frowned.

"What's the matter," Helen asked him.

"I'll tell you later," he replied. And then, to Adam, "Show me where this lady was when you saw her." They left the utility room and ventured outside onto the patio area, where Adam gestured to a spot in the garden where a weeping willow stood, beneath which was a set of wrought iron furniture.

"She was sitting at the table under the tree," said Adam.

"Stay here," Tim instructed and went to investigate.

On his return he shrugged and said, "She's nowhere to be seen. I guess she must've got bored and left."

To Adam he said, "If she returns, let me or your mother know straight away."

Adam promised that he would.

Later that day, Adam wandered into the garage where Tim was helping Helen unpack removal boxes. He was holding a figurine of a pretty Victorian lady.

"What do you have there?" Tim asked, going to him.

"The old woman gave it to me," said Adam.

"When?"

"Just."

"I thought I told you not to talk to her."

Adam looked confused. "That's not quite what you said, dad. You told me to tell her to talk to you if she wanted to come into the house. And that's what I did. And then she gave me this ornament, and walked off."

"If she tries to give you anything else," Helen said, "don't accept it. Okay?"

"But it's rude not to accept a gift from someone," Adam challenged.

"From someone you know, maybe," Helen said, "But not from perfect strangers. That's the golden rule, so stick to it. Is that clear, young man?"

"Yes," said Adam, looking suitably chastised.

Helen's demeanour softened. "Now, give me the ornament," she said holding out a hand.

Adam did as he was told.

Helen ruffled his blonde locks and said, "Good boy, now scoot."

"Do you think we've been too hard on him?" Helen asked Tim once he'd gone.

"We've acted in his best interests just like we always do," Tim said.

That evening, with Adam asleep in his bedroom, Helen quizzed Tim on the subject of the old woman, "You've seen her too, haven't you?" she said.

Tim nodded.

"When?"

Tim filled her in on the details, seeing no reason not to.

"Who is she, what does she want?" Helen asked.

"How should I know?"

"Whoever she is, I don't want her approaching my son again."

"You think I do?"

The following morning Tim was cutting the front lawn when he received a visit from his new neighbour.

"Michael Brown," the man said introducing himself and extending a hand for Tim to shake. He was a big, friendly individual, with grey, close cropped hair and a neatly clipped moustache. Tim took him to be in his mid sixties, and liked him immediately.

"Tim Christopher; pleased to meet you," Tim said shaking hands.

"Settling in okay?" Michael asked.

"There's a lot to do, but we're looking forward to the challenge," Tim said.

They continued passing the time of day up until the moment Helen appeared at the front door calling for Tim to come quickly. Tim excused himself and hurried into the house. He found Helen in the living room. Visibly shaken, she explained that she'd been in the kitchen moments before, organising the cupboards and drawers, when she happened to turn to face the window overlooking the back garden to be confronted by the sight of a hunched figure sitting at the patio table.

"It was the old woman you and Adam have seen, she fits the description perfectly, right down to the walking stick," Helen insisted, "I rushed outside to find out what she thought she was playing at, but by the time I got there she was gone. It was really creepy, Tim, she was just sitting there, as still as a statue, staring straight at me."

"Looks like we might have a problem," Tim commented.

"An understatement." Helen replied, "The question is; what on earth do we do about it?"

"We try to talk to the old dear," Tim reasoned. "Find out what she wants."

"Where's Adam?" Helen suddenly asked. "Have you seen him recently?"

"Not since breakfast," Tim said.

Helen rushed from the room, calling their son's name. She found him safe and sound in his bedroom playing on his computer.

"I suddenly had this awful thought that he'd been harmed in some way," Helen later explained to Tim.

"It's understandable," he said, "but we're talking about an old woman here, Helen. It's doubtful she'd have the strength to do anything untoward to Adam, or anyone else for that matter."

"Nevertheless," Helen said, and left it at that.

xx

Later that week, Helen came to Tim holding an old chipped vase in her hands.

"I thought we were through with buying junk from charity shops," Tim remarked when he saw it.

"I didn't buy it," Helen replied. "I found it."

"Where did you find it?"

"Standing on the dining table."

"How did it get there?"

"I was rather hoping you could tell me," Helen said, studying the object with mild suspicion.

Tim tried to make light of it. "Perhaps the old woman snuck in and put it there," he said with a theatrical shudder.

"Don't say that," Helen snapped back. "It's not funny."

Tim apologised. Helen walked off holding the vase at arm's length, as if it was something slightly dangerous.

xx

"Thought it might come in handy," Michael Brown said when Tim answered the front door the next morning. He was holding a Dewalt drill in his big gnarled hand.

"That's very good of you," Tim replied.

"Think nothing of it," Michael said, "I take it you still haven't found yours amongst the packing boxes?"

"Not yet," Tim said, "When do you need it back?"

"Keep it as long as you want," Michael insisted. "I've got a spare one I can use."

"Thanks, I appreciate it."

Michael jabbed a thumb back over his shoulder, in the direction of the nature reserve. "Just for your information, Tim, there exists around here a select little club affectionately called "Friends of the Reserve". We locals are proud of the place and meet over there on the last Sunday morning of every month. It's totally informal.

Members do a tidy up if it's required, take photo's... make sketches; some even draw enough inspiration to write poetry. It's a great way to get to know the neighbours Tim, so if you and your family find yourselves at a loose end, you'd be more than welcome to attend."

"Thanks," Tim said, meaning it. "We may take you up on your offer."

At that point Helen appeared at Tim's side.

Tim introduced her to their new neighbour.

"Pleased to meet you," Helen said.

Michael smiled. "Like-wise. Hope to see you both on Sunday," he said before wandering off in the direction of his house.

"What's happening on Sunday?" Helen asked.

Tim explained. "We should make the effort and go along," he suggested.

The Sunday morning gathering consisted of a dozen or so residents from the immediate surrounding area, one of whom was Michael's brother, Benjamin, who was the long serving parish vicar.

"I understand you're the proud new owners of "The Birches,"' Benjamin said to Tim and Helen following introductions. And then to Adam, "Do you like your new house, son?" Adam said he did, very much, and wandered off to chat to a lad of similar age.

The adults left him to it and took to exploring the reserve, making small talk as they went. As they entered a shaded copse, Helen suddenly broached the subject of the "The Birches" unwanted visitor.

"I don't think this is the right time," Tim interrupted, but she politely overrode him.

"We've been visited by an elderly lady," she informed the two men. "She keeps popping up in the grounds surrounding the house. We've twice found her sitting in the back garden. Have you any idea who she might be?"

Michael exchanged a puzzled look with his brother, who asked for a description. Tim obliged. The brothers exchanged another look. Benjamin went to speak but Michael beat him to it. "Can't think who that might be, I'm afraid."

Later that day, back at the house, Adam came indoors from the garden with another figurine.

"How did you come by that?" Helen immediately wanted to know. "Did the old woman give it to you? I thought we told you never to accept gifts from strangers, especially her."

"She didn't give it to me," Adam remonstrated. "I found it."

"Where?" asked Tim, who joined them having overheard the conversation.

"By the back door," Adam explained.

"Let me see it," Helen said, extending a hand. Adam gave it to her and she briefly inspected it. It was much like the first one Adam had brought into the house, being a delicate porcelain figure, this time portraying a young lady in a long bustle skirt and sun hat. The underside of the figurine's base was inscribed with words rendered illegible by age.

"What goes on, Tim?" Helen asked once Adam was out of the room. "Adam maintains the old woman gave him the first figurine and swears he found the second one outside. But what of the vase...how did that get into the house if we three didn't bring it in? I'm worried that the old woman really did sneak in here with it."

"Adam brought the vase into the house," Tim admitted. "I didn't tell you because I felt he's been berated quite enough already."

Helen grudgingly took his point. "But don't you dare keep me in the dark again. Do you understand?"

Tim offered an apology.

"Apology accepted," Helen said and pecked him on the check.

"Can we crack on with the unpacking now?"

"Is that all you ever think about, Tim Christopher?"

"What else is there?" he said, leaving the room bound for the garage.

xx

Michael called round unexpectedly the following day while Helen was in town doing the weekly shop.

"To what do I owe this pleasure," Tim asked upon answering the knock at the door.

"Mind if we talk," Michael asked.

Tim invited him in.

Over coffee in the dining room Michael said, "I didn't want to say anything in front of Helen the other day. She seemed a little bit stressed if you don't mind me saying."

"It's her workload combined with the house project," Tim explained, but that was only partly true. Helen was finding the unwanted sporadic appearances of the old woman distressing and made her fear for Adam's safety. She'd turned up unannounced again yesterday. Helen, who had spotted her in the back garden from an upstairs window, had rushed outside with the intention of confronting her, only to find her gone by the time she got there.

"She's freaking me out!" Helen had ranted at Tim upon his return home from work that afternoon.

It now appeared that Michael was about to impart information about her that Tim was unsure he wanted to hear.

"The description you gave the other day of your uninvited guest," he began, "You may as well have been describing Mrs Hargreaves."

Tim frowned. "You mean the previous owner of "The Birches"?

"The very same," Michael acknowledged.

"But we understood she sold the place in order to take up residence in a private nursing home."

"That was my understanding," Michael agreed. "Her family made her sell. They maintained she was no longer fit to live on her own. They were probably right, too. She was in pretty poor health. Trouble was she didn't want to go. She'd lived at "The Birches" all her married life. She was determined to stay, and by all accounts she put up a heck of a fight to do it, but in the end the family got its way."

"But why would she return here," Tim questioned.

"Perhaps she's home sick," Michael ventured.

"It can't possibly be Mrs Hargreaves," Tim insisted. "It doesn't make any sense."

"I agree," said Michael.

xx

That afternoon Tim arrived back from the DIY store to find Helen quizzing Adam.

"Where did you get it?" she asked as Tim entered the room. "I demand that you tell me."

Adam looked close to tears.

"The old woman told me to bring it in," he admitted. "She frightens me. I didn't want to upset her by refusing."

He looked across at the table upon which stood yet another figurine.

"I'm fed up with this nonsense," Helen said, looking at Tim. "What on earth is going on?" Without waiting for an answer she snatched the figurine off the table and left the room, headed for the kitchen.

"What are you going to do with it?" Tim called after her.

"Same thing I did with the others and the stupid vase," she answered back, "I'm going to bin it!"

"You can't do that," Tim said, chasing after her. "It's not your property!"

Helen turned on him. "I know damn well it's not mine! I also know I didn't ask for it or the other objects to be brought into my house. They have no place here so I'm getting rid. If the old hag doesn't like it, tough! She should've thought about that before she got our son to bring the blessed things in. And that's another thing. Who the hell does she think she is, coercing our son into such behaviour?" Helen was shaking with anger.

Tim went to her and pulled her close. "Hey, steady on," he said soothingly, "She's just an old misguided woman who wants to bring us moving in presents."

"If that's the case," Helen said, breaking the embrace, "Why doesn't she simply approach us with them herself, instead of skulking around."

Tim had no answer. Moreover, he was concerned by the fact that the old woman might be Mrs Hargreaves.

Later, in the study, Tim rifled through the red box folder that contained the conveyance information they'd amassed in order to purchase "The Birches". Rummaging through the paperwork he eventually came upon what he was looking for. It was the piece of paper containing the contact details of Mrs Hargreaves' son, who'd acted for his mother throughout the sale process.

Tim picked up the phone and dialled the man's number. Paul Hargreaves answered after three rings. Tim reintroduced himself and explained the reason he was phoning. There followed a long awkward silence before, finally, Paul Hargreaves said, "Is this some kind of sick joke Mr Christopher?"

Tim, taken aback by the response, replied, "No, Mr Hargreaves, this is simply a process of elimination. An elderly lady has taken it upon herself to hang around the house. We've been told she fits your mother's description."

There followed another lengthy silence.

"Mr Hargreaves, are you still there?" Tim was finally forced to ask.

"Yes, I'm still here," came the guarded reply.

"And?"

"The lady in question can't be my mother Mr Christopher, because my mother is dead."

Tim was too shocked to speak.

"She passed on within days of leaving "The Birches". She's dead and buried, Mr Christopher. I hope that answers your query. Goodbye."

The line went dead. Tim sat in stunned silence. Dead, Mrs Hargreaves was dead, he thought numbly, so the woman pestering them couldn't possibly be her. So who in God's name was she?

XX

"That's terrible," Michael said when Tim relayed the news to him. "The move was obviously too much for her."

"That's not all," Tim went on. From the back pocket of his jeans he produced a crumpled old monochrome photograph. He held it out for his neighbour to see. "I found it when I was ripping out an old wall unit in the utility room."

"That's Mrs Hargreaves," Michael said without hesitation.

"I guessed as much," said Tim. "It is also a picture of the woman who's been tormenting us since we first moved here."

Michael looked from Tim to the picture, then back to Tim again. "How can that be?"

"You tell me. I've kept all this from Helen. It would freak her out. I'm worried Mike. I don't believe in the hereafter, and all that goes with it, but neither can I explain any of what's happened through rational logic. It appears that we, and I mean Helen, Adam and I, keep seeing a woman walking around who passed on weeks ago. And then there's the other stuff..."

"What other stuff?" Michael asked.

Tim told him about the objects the old woman coerced Adam into bringing into the house.

"A vase, figurines, ornamental junk," Tim said.

Michael frowned. "I don't want to spook you any more than you already are, Tim, but Mrs Hargreaves late husband owned a porcelain factory. Mrs Hargreaves was a fanatical collector of figurines and vases."

Tim felt the blood drain from his face. "Anything else you want to tell me about the late Mrs Hargreaves?"

Michael ignored the question and said, "I think you might want to have a chat with my brother, Tim. Tell him what you've told me. You may be interested to hear what he has to say."

"You think so?"

Michael nodded. "I know so."

xx

That night, Helen was woken by noises coming from downstairs. She nudged Tim awake.

"Someone is in the house," she told him, keeping her voice low.

They got up and crept downstairs into the kitchen and through to the utility room, where they were alarmed to discover that the door leading outside was open.

"Stay here," Tim instructed and went to investigate, only to return moments later with nothing to report.

Back in the kitchen Helen drew Tim's attention to the hall. "Someone is in the front room," she whispered.

Tim grabbed a carving knife from the kitchen drawer. "Just in case," he said noticing the look of alarm on Helen's face.

They made their way quietly along the hall with Tim leading the way. At the door to the front room they paused and listened, but heard nothing. Tim, still holding the knife, stepped forward, and pushed the door ajar.

They entered the room to find Adam slumped against the wall, surrounded by countless porcelain figurines, vases and an array of other ornaments. Helen immediately rushed over to him, while Tim stared out through the big bay window, convinced he could see the old woman lurking outside in the darkness.

xx

60

"Adam doesn't remember anything about tonight, does he?" Helen asked Tim once Adam was safely returned to his bed.

"No," Tim said, "And perhaps that's just as well."

"The old woman is making him do things against his will," Helen said. "She's exerting some kind of control over him. At this rate she's going to scare us out of house, and home. What are we going to do, Tim?"

"I don't know," he said, but that wasn't true for he had already decided on the course of action to take. He just didn't want his wife to know.

xx

"She wants the house back."

Tim regarded the vicar with shocked disbelief.

"Are you serious?" He looked across the table at Michael.

"Is he serious?"

Michael nodded his head. "Ben never ever jokes about such matters."

They were in the drawing room at the vicarage. Michael had arranged the meeting between Tim and his brother following Tim's revelations about the ever deteriorating situation at "The Birches".

"She appears to be unable or unwilling to let go," Benjamin was saying.

"Are you trying to tell me she is a ghost," Tim asked; his sense of unease deepening.

"Based on what you and my brother have so far told me," said Benjamin, "it would appear that the late Mrs Hargreaves spirit is not yet at peace."

"Do you truly believe that?" Tim asked.

Benjamin considered the question carefully before answering. Finally, he said, "You have given me the facts, Tim, and in return I am giving you the only logical explanation available. It's up to you to decide whether my evaluation is correct or not, and then act accordingly."

Tim was silent for a long time, finding it virtually impossible to reconcile himself to the statement. He couldn't argue with the summation because the evidence really did point to their uninvited visitor being Mrs Hargreaves, and if Mrs Hargreaves was dead, which according to her son, she was; then the visitor must be her ghost.

"The vases and the figurines," Benjamin said, "suggest she is attempting to repossess the house. She appears to be moving her personal effects in, Tim, using your son as an unwitting collaborator. Children are psychically gifted to a high degree. Your son will be naturally receptive to the spirit's suggestions and instructions. It seems she has gained his trust, or else made him too afraid to refuse."

"But the objects we're talking about are real," Tim interrupted. "How can that possibly be?"

"Psychical manifestations," Benjamin explained, "can appear to be very real. The spirit is exerting its will over you and your family, persuading you to believe in its existence in a physical sense. A lot depends on the spirit's level of determination as to how successful it is in achieving its goal. What we have here Tim is an escalating battle of wills. The outcome will depend on whose will is stronger, yours or that of the spirit."

"You're saying, not only do spirits exist," said Tim, "but they can also alter an individual's perception of reality."

Benjamin nodded. "I am indeed."

Tim looked at Michael, who stared impassively.

"So what do you suggest we do to remedy the situation?" Tim asked the vicar.

"You have certain options available to you," he replied. "You can leave "The Birches" and allow the spirit to reclaim the house, or you can simply live with the situation and deal with events as they unfold. In other words, treat the spirit as an unwanted guest."

"Impossible," Tim interjected.

"Or," Benjamin continued unabashed, "You can fight to regain full ownership of the house."

"And how do you propose we do that?" Tim asked sceptically, whilst struggling to make sense of all he was hearing.

"You either hold a séance," Benjamin said, "or you call in a holy person to perform an exorcism."

Tim felt his jaw drop. He was beginning to feel genuinely afraid for himself and his family.

"Which avenue would you chose?" he asked looking at both men in turn, unable to make a decision for himself.

"The latter two options are fraught with a certain element of danger," said the vicar. "Things can go wrong."

"In what way?"

"Should the spirit be angered by the process, and manages to exert its will," Benjamin explained, "Things can get pretty hairy."

"You have personal experience of this?" Tim asked.

Benjamin shook his head.

"Who do you know that does?"

"I would have to consult with my colleagues," Benjamin admitted. "Genuine paranormal activity is extremely rare. What I do know is that your spirit is unable to gain access to your house, due to the death of its physical self taking place elsewhere. This fact gives you and your family an advantage. It is also why the spirit is using your son as an agent. A word of warning; under no circumstances invite the spirit into the house itself, as that will allow it to gain full possession of the property."

"Are we in immediate danger?" Tim asked.

The brothers glanced at each other.

"Depends," said Benjamin.

"Upon what?" asked Tim.

"Upon what kind of person Mrs Hargreaves was in life."

Tim looked from Benjamin to Michael. "Do we know?" he asked feeling a sudden unexplained rush of apprehension.

Michael spoke. "Mrs Hargreaves went through a particularly bad spell not long after she moved into "The Birches". She was pregnant and gave birth to twin boys, but the experience brought on mental collapse, which resulted in a terrible tragedy." Michael glanced nervously over at his brother who continued with the account. "There's no easy way to say this," the vicar began. "As Michael rightly said, Mrs Hargreaves suffered a breakdown, which led her to conclude that her twin boys were possessed by evil spirits."

"What happened?" Tim demanded to know.

"She decided to drown the boys in order to cleanse their souls," Benjamin said. "One survived, the other perished. The surviving child was taken into care whilst Mrs Hargreaves was placed in a psychiatric unit for a period of time before finally being allowed home, where she lived until you bought the house."

"Why didn't you tell me this before," Tim asked Michael as he got up to leave.

"Because I didn't want to worry you," Michael replied.

"Didn't want to worry me," Tim exploded, "How the hell do you think I feel now!"

xx

Back at "The Birches", Helen stood in the front room shaking from head to toe, her faced drained of all colour. All her possessions were gone, replaced by furniture and ornaments she failed to recognise. Worse was the fact that the old woman was present in the room. She's moved in, Helen thought with total disbelief, and knew instinctively that the house was lost to them forever.

"Helen, I have to talk to you!" a voice suddenly declared from behind.

She spun round to see Tim standing in the doorway.

"Oh my God, no," he said when he saw who else occupied the room

"Adam must've let her in," Helen said, her voice shaking uncontrollably.

"Where is he," Tim yelled at the intruder, "Where is my son, what have you done to him!?"

The answer he sought poured from the mouth of the old woman like poison.

"He's in the bath, my dear, having his sins washed away."

xx

Headline taken from "The Stallington Chronicle" later that year...

"Husband and wife convicted of the manslaughter of their seven year old son on the grounds of diminished responsibility."

xx

65

Extract from the transcript of police statement, ref 621, made by Benjamin Brown, vicar of Stallington Parish in the presence of D. I. Simon Davis and D. S. Scott Yates.

BB: The couple thought they were haunted by the spirit of "The Birches" previous owner. The husband visited me seeking advice on behalf of himself and his family.

SD: What advice did you give?

BB: I offered options and tried to reassure."

SY: Can you be more specific?

BB: The possibilities of holding a séance and performing an exorcism were discussed.

SD: Nothing more?

BB: No.

SD: And this conversation took place on the day Adam Christopher died.

BB: Correct.

xx

The young couple loved "The Birches" but expressed initial concerns about its violent history.

"I can live with its past if you can," the husband declared to his wife during a revisit.

"I must admit, it's an incredible amount of house for the money," she said, finally warming to the idea. "What do you think, Alice," she asked their six year old daughter, "shall we buy it?"

"Can we," asked the child, "It'd be fun living in a haunted house."

CLOSE CALL

Hi, my name is Amy, I'm a twenty-five-year old legal secretary, and this is my story. One evening while I was out socialising with friends, I met a man called David. A school teacher in his late twenties, he was handsome, intelligent and fun loving. He also happened to be single. Within minutes, he had swept me off my feet. Following a whirlwind courtship, we became engaged. He proposed on Valentine's Day. It was one of the happiest days of my life.

David still lived at home with his parents, but assured me that he was saving hard for a deposit to buy a place of his own. At the time I was fortunate to be a house owner already, an achievement of which I was extremely proud. When David asked me to sell my little corner of England so we might buy a property jointly, I guess it was only natural that I harboured misgivings.

I felt I would be giving up my independence and in doing so, might make myself vulnerable. Yet wasn't David the man I had agreed to marry, I asked myself. Wasn't he the man whom I loved, and whose children I so dearly wanted? Surely, being married to him would make my life complete and make up in part for the fact that I had no close family of my own. And so it was that I agreed to sell my pride and joy and move in temporarily with his parents, while we searched for a place we could call our own.

I had met them once previously. The meeting was brief and rather awkward, as such meetings invariably are. His father was a catering manager and struck me as being a timid man with little to say. His mother by sharp contrast, was outgoing with a forceful personality; an attractive woman for her age. Glamorous and theatrical, she reminded me of the actress—Joan Collins. It was immediately apparent that she doted on her son to the point of fanaticism, praising him constantly, bragging about how she cleaned, ironed and cooked for him. Despite this, I never once regarded David as a mummy's boy. Quite the contrary, for he seemed to know his own mind and held strong opinions which he wasn't afraid to air whenever the opportunity arose. I couldn't help but notice however, that he trod carefully around his mother, as if afraid to upset her.

My house sold quickly, a fact I found disappointing, for I'd hoped for a little time, a breathing space that would enable me to persuade David to set up home there instead. It was with some reluctance, therefore, that I started to pack and make removal arrangements.

David suggested we take his parents out to dinner so we could start getting to know each other. It was an unmitigated disaster. His father said barely a word all night, while his mother dominated the conversation, and proved to be a self- opinionated bore. She tended to treat her husband like a fool and David like a little boy. Most worrying was the fact that David and his father failed to question her behaviour. I quickly concluded that David's mother was a bully, his father a coward. I found it impossible to warm to them. What on earth had I been thinking about in agreeing to share their home? Had it not been for the fact that my house sale had reached the point of no return, with removals and storage booked and paid for, I may well have cancelled the arrangement.

I next saw them three weeks later, on my birthday. To celebrate, the four of us dined out at a lovely country restaurant. Much to my relief David's father proved more inclined to initiate conversation on this occasion, and while his mother was her usual overbearing self she was at least tolerable. Until that is, the men disappeared to the bar to order fresh drinks. While they were away, she offered me some words of advice.

"It would be best for all concerned if you saw less of David," she told me bluntly. When I asked her why, she simply replied, "If you must know, I'm not entirely convinced you're right for him."

In bed that night, David remarked that I seemed a little bit down. An understatement if ever there was one. I felt distraught. I thought about telling him what his mother had said, but decided not to rock the boat in the hope that time would make his mother realise she was wrong about me.

The dreaded day came when I was to move out of my beloved house and into my new home. I'd been there only once before and recalled it being bigger than it actually was. We found living together a squeeze right from the start, which created tension. On top of that, David's mother felt the need to constantly compete with me for her son's affections, while his father seemed to find my presence an intrusion into his mundane life. But it was his mother's mood swings that really worried me. One moment she could be as nice as pie, the next she was cruel and vindictive. Alcohol, which played a large part in her life, made her dangerously unpredictable. Regardless of her mood, or whether or not she was inebriated, I tried to keep out of her way as much as possible.

One Sunday morning, David and I were rudely awoken by the sound of knocking at the bedroom door. It was his mother announcing that someone called Stacy was here to see David.

"Who's Stacy?" I asked, bleary-eyed.

"An old friend," David said, flustered "I haven't seen her for months. God only knows what she's doing calling round now."

I was suddenly wide awake with alarm bells ringing in my head, "An old friend, as in girlfriend?" I asked.

Before he could reply, there was another knock at the door. "David," his mother cooed from the other side, "Stacy is waiting."

"It's inconvenient," he said with a notable lack of conviction. "Tell her I'll call her later."

"Oh no, you won't," I said feeling deeply upset.

"She's made a special trip," his mother said through the door. "Come along, David. She's waiting."

David obediently jumped out of bed and started to dress.

"What are earth do you think you're doing?" I asked incredulously.

"Don't worry, I won't be long," he said sheepishly as he hurried from the room. I watched him go, feeling confused and threatened by the turn of events. I wanted to find out exactly what was going on, and who the mysterious Stacy was, but part of me felt it would be intruding. I tried to shrug the whole thing off and get back to sleep, but sleep was impossible, so I lay there feeling miserable.

David later explained that Stacy was the ex-girlfriend of Carl, an old friend of his, and that they'd kept in touch on and off since her relationship with Carl had ended.

"It was a bit of a coincidence that she turned up out of the blue like she did," I said.

David shrugged it off as one of those things and I grudgingly let the matter drop.

Over the next couple of weeks, David and I house hunted intensely. We spoke to estate agents and viewed potentially suitable properties but nothing we saw set our imaginations on fire. Then, one night as I scoured the local paper, I spotted a lovely cottage situated on the outskirts of town. It was exactly the type of house I had always dreamed of owning. Although the price was at the top of our range, I was prepared to make the sacrifices necessary to secure it. David however, wasn't so sure.

"But it's just what we've been looking for," I said. "Can't we at least view it?"

Reluctantly, David agreed. By now I was desperate for us to find a place of our own. Living with David's parents was intolerable. His mother, I had decided, was emotionally unstable, being friendly to a fault one moment and openly hostile the next. Furthermore, she had an unsettling habit of following me around the house whilst talking incessantly to me, forever mentioning the mysterious Stacy, how Stacy was such a nice girl, and how much David thought of her. Eventually, the constant references to Stacy overwhelmed me and I confronted David on the matter.

"Just who the hell is she?" I demanded to know.

"Just a friend," he maintained.

I could tell he was lying and he knew it.

"Who is she?!" I repeated angrily.

He finally came clean. "I dated her briefly after she split with Carl. It didn't work out and we went our separate ways."

"How come she suddenly turned up at the house that day?

"I don't know."

"You're lying."

"Mum asked her to come over."

I was devastated. "Why, for God's sake?"

"I have no idea."

But I did. David's mother saw Stacy as David's ideal partner, rather than me, and was intent on taking steps to achieve that end.

"Promise me you won't see Stacy ever again, or we're finished," I said, meaning it. David promised. "And tell your mother to stop tormenting me by mentioning her name all the time," I added.

David said that he would.

If he did, it failed to have the desired effect. The references to Stacy continued unabated. The battle of wills between David's mother and I also continued. I would make sandwiches for him to take to work. Trouble was, so would she. Inevitably, David would end up accepting both prepared lunches just to keep the peace. I occasionally wondered which sandwiches he enjoyed more, his mother's or mine.

Time went by, but the situation in the household didn't improve. The tension between David's parents and I grew unbearable. Eventually I confided in David, saying that I found it all too much of a strain living with his family and wanted us to move out. I thought he would understand. Instead, he took offence and defended them.

"I think you're being ungrateful," he said stubbornly. "They've really put themselves out so we can stay with them, you know."

I found myself apologising, when I really wanted to tell him to wake up to the fact that he had an unstable mother and, dare I say it, a peeping tom for a father. I had no proof of the latter, just a sneaky suspicion his father was prone to spying on me. I'd initially told myself it was all in my head. Then, one day, upon returning to the house unexpectedly, having forgotten some work papers, I found him in my room. "David's mother wondered if the boy had any clothes ready for the wash," he said by way of explanation. Afterwards I happened to notice the drawer containing my lingerie was partly open, though whether it was coincidence or not, I'll never know.

The following weekend, we viewed the house I had set my heart on buying. It was everything I'd hoped it would be, a little bit on the small side perhaps, but that I could live with. The positives far outweighed the negatives. It was in close proximity to both our places of work, was convenient for local amenities, had a lovely big mature garden and best of all, it had a conservatory. It was my dream-come true.

David, however, was less than enthusiastic. When pressed, he came up with weak objections for not wanting to purchase the property. It was too much for our pocket, he said. I reminded him that we had already discussed price and agreed that it would be worth the extra outlay. It needed too much work, he complained. I pointed out that the house was fully renovated. He came back at me arguing it would require too much general maintenance. I couldn't win. David's negative attitude left me unhappy and disillusioned. David treated me to dinner at a posh restaurant by the river in an attempt to cheer me up. He tried his best to reassure me by saying he wanted the same things that I did, that he only had my best interests at heart.

"If we're patient, we'll find a better house," he assured me.

"But I don't want a better house," I replied adamantly. "I want the one we've just seen!"

"It's wrong for us," he said. "Mum agrees."

So that was it, I thought angrily. His mother had voiced her opposition and turned David against it. Only it wasn't the house she didn't like, it was me! Moreover, she didn't want her precious son to leave the nest and spread his wings, unless of course it was with the fantastic Stacy!

We walked straight into a blazing row on our return from the restaurant that night. David's mother had expected us back in time to join her and her boring husband for the evening meal. She had cooked especially, she said, in celebration of the fact that we were all getting along so well. I almost laughed aloud at the irony. She accused me of leading David astray, of making him behave inconsiderately.

"I bet Stacy would never behave inappropriately," she said pointedly to David. "She's such a lovely girl, son. Why she isn't married yet, I'll never know."

At that point, I decided I'd had enough. I also realised David's mother had been drinking again. Some might argue that the alcohol was responsible for releasing the vicious barb in her tongue, though I'm of the opinion that what is said under the influence is invariably heartfelt. Nevertheless, I tried to reason with her, but only succeeded in antagonising her further. I looked to David and his father to intervene, but they did nothing. Finally, unable to cope any longer, I fled from the house with David hot footing it after me.

"Come back inside," he urged, catching up with me at the garden gate.

"Not until your mother apologises for her behaviour," I said tearfully.

"She won't," he said with absolute certainty. "Believe it or not, she does mean well, you know."

"She's got a pretty strange way of showing it," I retorted. I tried to walk away, but David gently restrained me by the shoulders and said, "She shouldn't drink. She's all right until she drinks. Dad and I have both tried to explain to her what she's like when she does, but it does no good."

"Maybe you should video her," I said sarcastically. "If she saw what she's like for herself, I doubt she'd ever touch alcohol again."

"That's as maybe," said David calmly, "but it isn't going to happen."

"Why didn't you warn me what she can be like, David?"

"I didn't think there would be a problem," he said lamely. Then he smiled and suggested we go for a drive so we might discuss things and hopefully resolve the situation.

"The only way to do that," I said, "is to buy a place of our own and move out."

We went for the drive anyway. Nothing was resolved. In fact, it only made matters worse. David made the mistake of confiding that his mother had a history of depressive illness. The information only went to confirm my worst fears.

"Has she ever been violent?" I asked dreading the reply. David changed the subject, which only went to increase my concern.

We were away from the house less than one hour. When we arrived back, it was to find that we were locked out. David's key refused to work suggesting the catch had been slipped from the inside. We rang the front door bell and knocked the door, all to no avail.

"What's going on, David?" I asked. "What do we do now? In case you had forgotten, we both have work in the morning and nowhere to sleep and nothing to sleep in."

David gazed around uncertainly, as if hoping an answer to our dilemma might appear out of thin air. Then, in subdued silence he walked back to the car. At a loss to know what else to do, I followed.

We spent the next hour driving around like idiots trying to find a cheap hotel room for the night, but had absolutely no success. In the end, and with it being way past midnight, we were forced to book into a more expensive establishment out of sheer desperation. So, with no overnight belongings to speak of, we moved in and went straight to bed. Less than an hour later I was wide awake, suffering from stomach cramps. I woke David with my tossing and turning. He tried to comfort me in his own manly way by offering to call for a doctor, unaware that a doctor was the last thing I needed. I knew perfectly well what was wrong. It was that time of the month, wouldn't you just know it! I ended up lying awake for most of the night, whilst wishing a thousand painful deaths upon David's mother.

In the morning, at first light, we left the hotel and returned to David's parents' house. This time, miraculously, David's key worked, and we crept into the hall like a pair of naughty school children, both of us I suspect bitterly afraid of incurring the wrath of David's mother for the second time in as many days. Instead, we met with his father, who mumbled a half-hearted apology for the fact that we had been locked out, and quickly disappeared upstairs with two steaming cups of tea.

By now, I was incredulous of the situation I had managed to get myself into. My stay at David's parent's house was turning into a living nightmare. Worse was the fact that there didn't appear to be a way out. We had yet to find an alternative place to live, due mainly to David's reluctance. In the meantime we both found ourselves treading on eggshells, afraid of upsetting David's mother still further. I felt well and truly trapped. I could barely believe that less than two months earlier I was a young independent working girl with my own house, and my own uncomplicated life. Now I'd been relegated to the role of lodger whose landlady appeared to be some kind of latent psychopath. When two days later I emerged unsuspectingly from the bathroom wearing nothing but a towel to find David's maniacally grinning mother loitering on the landing with the offer of a cup of tea, I was finally forced to admit I would have to make arrangements to leave.

That night I had a frank discussion with David, wherein I pleaded that he tell his mother we had decided to rent a property until such time we found one we liked enough to buy. He was suitably empathetic and agreed it was probably for the best.

When, after a further two weeks, nothing happened, I issued David with an ultimatum, demanding he do the unthinkable and choose between his mother and me. His reaction shocked me, for he started to cry.

"I can't hurt her like that," he blubbered. "Not after all that she's done for me."

He begged me to give him a little more time and promised that we would intensify our search for a house. And initially, he kept his promise. He helped me scour the property sections of local papers, visited estate agents' web sites and arranged numerous viewings on an endless list of properties, all with great enthusiasm. But of course it all came to nothing, just as I knew it would, for David had no real intention of leaving the family fold. He wanted everything to remain as it was, and for me to live with him and his mother and father, happily ever after. I was at my wit's end, with no one to turn to for help.

A further three weeks dragged painfully by, during which time David's mother grew increasingly hostile and antagonistic towards me. The further deterioration in our relationship left me utterly mystified. I tried to discuss the situation with David. During the conversation he let slip that he had told her about my ultimatum.

"But your mother was the reason I gave you the ultimatum in the first place, you idiot!" I was at the end of my tether. "No wonder she's taken against me so. What on earth possessed you to do it?"

"I had no option," he said blandly. "She knew something was wrong. She always knows."

I despised him for his weakness of character. He was just like his father, I thought miserably—as spineless as a jellyfish. I felt betrayed and disillusioned, but most of all I felt isolated and alone. I looked at David that day, and instead of seeing someone to admire, I saw a coward.

I finally had to accept that the man I'd chosen to marry was firmly under his mother's thumb, and that the status quo would more than likely remain unchanged.

Regretfully, I decided to leave him. It was a painful decision to have to make and not one I took lightly. I had given up my home and my independence for David and spent over four miserable months in the company of people who, for reasons of their own, had taken an instant dislike to me. The night I broke the bad news to David was also the night that his mother discovered my intentions. David told her, of course. Being the perfect son, he was inclined to tell her everything.

She took the news badly.

Almost twelve months have passed since the knife attack and my subsequent fight for life. It was a close call, according to the doctors, very close. I had a lucky escape, they said. With hindsight, I can see that I also had a lucky escape in not marrying David. I thought I knew him well enough to know I'd be happy sharing the rest of my life with him. In reality, he turned out to be nothing like I thought. It just goes to show you can never be certain about anyone. He was a mummy's boy, and boy, what a mummy he had. Whether the experience has made me a stronger person is anyone's guess. All I know is, I'll make darned sure I take a long, hard look before I ever jump again. If of course, there is a next time.

WHO REMEMBERS WHO?

I'm in a local department store searching for my wife whom I seem to have mislaid between the never-ending rows of female fashion garments. I approach a shop assistant who is busy pretending to be busy, and I ask what appears to me to be a perfectly simple question.

"Do you happen to have seen my wife?"

The shop assistant stops what she's doing, which isn't very much, and frowns quizzically. "Your wife," she says cocking her head to one side. "I'm afraid I don't know your wife."

Now this is where it gets interesting, because I reply quite emphatically, "Ah, but you do. I saw you speaking with her just before..." and here I pause, uncertain what it is I wish to say next. The shop assistant observes me curiously, "Just before what?"

"Petite," I reply, deliberately avoiding the question, "with blonde hair and green eyes. She was wearing a blood red blouse. You and she were laughing as if you were sharing a private joke, and then," and here I pause again, once more unsure of what it is I want to say. The shop assistant is forced to prompt me a second time.

"And then what?" she asks with slight impatience.

Now I'm the one wearing the curious expression.

"You must remember my wife," I urge. "Just before whatever happened, happened, you turned to look at a woman who'd entered the store making a bit of a din, chanting something or other."

Comprehension fleetingly crosses the shop assistant's face and then it's gone, replaced by sudden confusion, and something else: is it fear I detect in her eyes?

"I remember now," I say shakily with the dawning realisation of what exactly has happened here. "I was walking towards you both. Like I said before, you were laughing, you and my wife: and then this woman enters the store, she looks out of it, kind of delirious and she's chanting gibberish. She's got her arms raised to the heavens, as if seeking divine guidance, and then, just before it happens and everything goes haywire, she drops her arms and fumbles inside her clothing for something. You and my wife were watching her, alarmed, in fact everyone was watching her, it was hard to ignore; she was making such a racket."

"Stop right there!" The shop assistant almost screams the words at me. The next thing I know, she's broken down in floods of tears.

"I don't want to know," she blubbers into a trembling hand.

"You remember, don't you?" I say, whilst I, too, try to come to terms with the reality of what's happened here in this very ordinary high street store.

The shop assistant has collapsed to her knees, crying and shrieking that it is all so unfair. She is absolutely distraught, and why wouldn't she be, I ask myself. I'm pretty upset too, it has to be said. I look around and suddenly, miraculously, I see my wife standing there. She wears a blank expression. She looks straight at me, but there's no recognition there, nothing, zilch. We might as well be perfect strangers. The shop assistant is still on her knees in front of me, head in hands, no longer shrieking, just quietly sobbing. And my wife, I call out to her, trying to keep my voice steady.

"Susie, over here—it's me, Phil!"

She continues to look, but doesn't seem to see me. It's like she's in shock and looking straight through me. Well, I guess that might well be the case, bearing in mind what's occurred. I go over to her, leaving the shop assistant alone with her feelings of devastation, and try to take Susie's hand.

"Who are you?" she asks, and I really can't believe my own ears.

"Susie, it's me, Phil, your husband."

Plainly, her mind is in no man's land. No recognition, no nothing. It's going to take time, but I guess we have quite a lot of that in light of recent events. I somehow manage to avert my gaze from Susie's eerily blank face and for the first time take in the horrific devastation surrounding us. The debris, the thick dust and dark acrid smoke, and of course, the bodies, mine and Susie's no doubt amongst them, lying somewhere in the rubble, together with that of the shop assistant's, I dare say.

I can see others now, wandering around aimlessly, the lost and confused, others, like Susie and I and the shop assistant, spectral remnants of the almighty bomb blast that killed us moments before we decided to forget to remember. But the amnesia won't last forever. Just like the shop assistant and I, Susie and all the other lost souls debilitated by shock, will eventually come round and be forced to accept the awful truth. And we'll all no doubt be asking the same unanswerable question: "Why?"

YOURS TRULY

It's my day off and I'm sitting in front of the TV watching a Seinfeld re-run. All of a sudden there's a knock at the front door. When I finally summon up the energy to answer it, I'm horrified to find it's yours truly standing there! Yeah, that's right; it's me, my own sweet self, who's staring back at me. I slam the door shut and slip the catch. Well, wouldn't you? I try to tell myself I imagined it. Stress, that's what it is—or maybe the booze? I'm rather partial to the odd tipple. Ignore it, yeah, that's what I'll do: I'll go back to watching the TV, pretend it never happened. I start to turn. Suddenly, there's another knock, louder than the first.

Christ! Someone really is out there! But it can't be me, because I'm here! Do I answer it? What if it is me, what then? Perhaps it's someone who happens to look like me: someone who is my absolute double: a long-lost twin, maybe? But the dude at the door is even wearing the same clothes as me! How can that happen? Another knock at the door, more insistent, spurs me into action. Whoever is there, (well, I know who's there, it's me, but I also know it's impossible for it to be me), has no intention of going away. Against my better judgement, I open the door for the second time in as many minutes. Yep, it's me all right, larger than life and twice as ugly.

"What do you want?" A reasonable question, yet it sounds quite ridiculous given the bizarre circumstances. Wouldn't I know what I want if it's me standing there?

My other self pipes up, saying, "They told me you were here."

"Who did?"

"The voices..."

"What voices?"

"The ones inside my head."

Alarm bells ring (not inside my head, I'm talking metaphorically here), and I'm thinking this guy, he's crazy, but he's also standing on my doorstep and I have to deal with him.

"These voices you hear," I say as calmly as I can, "What else did they tell you?"

"They gave me directions so I could find you."

"A bit like a Sat Nav?"

He frowns, contemplating. And it makes him look even more like me. Dad used to hate me frowning. "Don't frown," he'd say angrily. "It makes you look like a simpleton!" So I try never to frown, not that I have ever really believed frowning makes me look simple in any way, shape or form. However, I must say, looking at myself now, I kind of see what dad meant. Frowning makes me look as if I'm zoned out on drugs or something.

"Go away!" I say it as if I mean it.

He refuses to budge.

"I said, bugger off!"

Well, what else can a person say when they're confronted by their own sweet self. "Hi, come in, let's have a cup of tea and get to know each other." Of course not! How ludicrous! I already know myself perfectly well, thank you very much.

"We need to talk," he says, still frowning like a crack head.

"Oh no, we don't!"

"Oh yes, we do!"

Suddenly it's pantomime season!

"What's the point of talking," I ask, and he says, "I would have thought that was obvious. You're a doppelganger and you must leave immediately so I can get on with my life."

"What did you just call me?"

"A doppelganger: you're a doppelganger, my friend, and you're interfering with my life."

I can hardly believe my own ears. "I beg to differ. I'll have you know I'm no such thing." But I don't know what a doppelganger is, so how do I know I'm not one? So I ask the question.

"What's a doppelganger?"

He shakes his head at me like I'm...well...simple. And I'm not even frowning! Or am I? He is, I know that much. It makes him look dangerous.

"A doppelganger," he says in a snooty little voice that reminds me of...errrrm...me, "is a person's astral double. When someone meets their doppelganger, heaven forbid, problems occur. Things go awry. The only way to resolve the situation is for the doppelganger to leave."

"And if it won't leave?"

"It has to be made to leave."

Hang on a minute: he's accusing me of being the doppelganger. How do I know it isn't him? So I confront him with the question.

"How the dickens can I possibly be an astral body? I live in a house. I drive a car. I go to work. I have relatives and friends. I exist."

He shrugs, unimpressed. "So what? So do I."

"It's a stalemate, then."

He shakes his head. "Not quite."

"So why am I the doppelganger and not you?"

"It's really quite simple," he says with a smug little grin. "You're the doppelganger because the doppelganger is always unaware of its double."

He's got me. It seems he's won the argument—if that is, he's telling the truth. But what, I ask myself, would be the point of lying to myself?

"I suppose you'd better come in."

He walks past me into the hall. I quickly weigh him up. We're evenly matched physically speaking. Well, we would be, wouldn't we? I decide there's nothing else for it. It's a case of self-preservation. I prepare to make my move. As soon as his back is turned, I jump him. There's a fight. It's vicious, so vicious in fact; we end up knocking each other unconscious.

When I come round, he's nowhere to be seen, my other self, the doppelganger. He's left. It seems like I can get on with my life in peace. Or is it his life?

Now I come to think of it, I'm no longer sure which one of us did leave, me or him, him or me?

But does it really matter?

At least one of us is here.

BON APPETIT

He gets to the pub ahead of time, grabs a beer from the bar and settles down at a quiet corner table. And there he waits. His name is Steve or Stevie to his work colleagues and friends, Stephen to his overbearing mother. He's fast approaching thirty is Steve or Stevie or Stephen, and feels time is running out. He yearns for a steady relationship, maybe even a wife. The traditional way hasn't worked for him - he just can't seem to meet the right girl, meaning a looker with a servile demeanour, so about three months ago, he decided to go the cyber way.

Two failed liaisons later—one was plain speaking and ugly, the other was plain ugly and barely spoke—he thinks he might have hit the jackpot with Caroline. She's a singer and dancer, who is presently a secretary with a manufacturing firm. She doesn't like it much, she says; it's boring and her boss is a jerk, but she's prepared to put up with it until she gets her big break. She's twenty-four, is Caroline, sounds sweet as apple pie, and judging from her photo, she's a stunner, reminding Steve of Angelina Jolie.

Steve is sitting with his back to the blazing pub fire, gazing out of the window onto the car park, waiting expectantly for Caroline aka Angelina to show up. He sips nervously at his beer and resists the urge to nip outside for a crafty cigarette, he's told Caroline he's a non-smoker, and instead, contemplates the night to come. He has also told Caroline he is a construction site manager, which is another white lie; in truth, he earns a living from laying bricks, but he feels comfortable with the fibs he's told because he intends kicking the weed, and is convinced a career in site management is his for the taking. Like Caroline, all he needs is the right break and his career will soar into orbit. So they have something in common, it seems.

Steve checks his wristwatch. 7:59pm. One minute and then she will be late. Steve hates tardiness in a person. If Caroline is late, even by a second, it would be a bad start to what should be a promising liaison. Oh no, lateness would never do. Steve is a perfectionist. Everything in its place and a place for everything, is his motto. His flat is spotless. The food cans in his cupboards are always neatly lined up with the labels facing forwards. His shirts are neatly ironed and hang perfectly aligned in his wardrobe. Things have to be just right.

It's the same when it comes to bricklaying. Steve has yet to lay a brick incorrectly. The mortar has to be perfect in its consistency; the wall ties must be symmetrical even though they will never be seen once the building is complete. He gets it from his mother. When he was young, neatness was forever drilled into him. "Always put things away after you've used them, Stephen," his mother would say, just as cleanliness was drilled into him. "Cleanliness is next to Godliness," his mother repeatedly affirmed as she went about her daily housework. "Isn't that right, Stephen?" "Yes mum," he would agree, while watching her carefully out of the corner of his eye. She could be unpredictable. One moment she was his kind, good-hearted mother; the next a bullying stranger. Steve inherited her quick temper but controls it better...usually...

Steve is just about to check his watch again when he spots a car pull onto the pub car park. It's a red Ford Focus. It comes to a stop just outside the main door to the lounge where Steve presently sits cradling his half empty beer glass. A moment later the headlights go off and the car door opens and out steps a girl with long, auburn hair. She wears a sexy, figure-hugging dress and high heels. Steve straightens in his seat and licks his lips in anticipation. It's her! Jesus, she's actually turned up! He can hardly bring himself to believe it. And all this is happening thanks to the advert he placed on the webpage of an internet dating agency, an ill-conceived ad at that, which simply read, "Attractive twenty-nine-year old male seeks attractive, intelligent gal for fun nights out and in. Likes soccer, walking, reading and country walks. Contact..."

He hopes this is third time lucky. It certainly looks that way so far. The first two were stinkers, especially the second, with her gormless expression and piss poor conversation. He tries to recall her name: Jenny, or was it Penny? Time will tell with this one, he thinks as he watches the girl climb the short run of steps to the lounge bar entrance and disappear inside. When she enters the bar itself, Steve stands automatically. It's her all right, and she looks even better than her photo suggested. She is tall and statuesque. Her dark hair gleams. Her eyes sparkle. The dress she wears has a plunging neckline. A group of men at the bar turn to look, their eyes following her progress as she spots Steve and walks over.

Steve clears his throat to speak. "Caroline. It is you, isn't it?"

She smiles sweetly and joins him at the table.

"Hi Steve..." She extends a slender hand, rather formally, he thinks, but he shakes it anyway and gestures for her to sit.

"What's your poison?"

She asks for a dry white wine. He goes to the bar feeling as if he's walking on a cloud, he's so happy. Rod Stewart sings inside his head, "Tonight's the Night..." Sure is if he gets his way, he thinks as he pays the barman, and returns with Caroline's drink.

"Cheers," he says raising his beer glass, trying not to leer.

"Salute," she responds pleasantly. They sip their drinks and then Steve says, "I can't believe you're here. I mean, it's like wow!"

Caroline smiles her lovely smile. Her dark eyes twinkle with suppressed delight. "I've been looking forward to us meeting Steve. Really I have. We seem to click, if you know what I mean."

They make small talk for a while, appearing to relax in each other's company. Caroline offers to buy Steve another drink. He declines.

"It's the driving," he says.

"You don't have to worry about that," Caroline tells him.

"I don't?"

"Of course not; I'll be doing the driving tonight. I'm taking us back to my place, unless you have other plans?"

Steve gulps back his surprise. "That sounds good, Caroline," he says, unable to believe his luck.

"Hobbies," Caroline says as she rejoins him having purchased fresh drinks, an orange juice for her and a lager for him. "What did you say your hobbies were, Steve? I forget."

"Soccer, walking, having fun," he says smiling. "Oh, and I collect autographs; football players mainly."

Caroline smiles back. "I quite enjoy collecting things too: shoes, handbags; anything that grabs my interest. Take you for instance. You interest me greatly, Steve."

"I do?"

"Drink up, let's go."

Caroline's home is a revelation to Steve when he awakens from the sharp blow he has received to the head. The room he occupies is dark and squalid, illuminated by a single kerosene lamp. Broken furniture and rubbish fill the place. He tries to rise from his prone position on the bare concrete floor, but is prevented from doing so by the tight bindings around his hands and feet. Naked, he shivers uncontrollably. He wants to cry out but his mouth is gagged. Panic sets in and he struggles against the restraints, but to no avail. He feels groggy; his head throbs painfully.

"Help me," he cries out in his mind. "For God's sake, help me!" Of course, no one hears him because he is unable to speak. Caroline, he thinks as he starts to remember, where the hell are you, you bitch?" He vaguely recalls being driven to a house; isolated, rundown. He entered first at Caroline's behest, heard Caroline close the door behind him, and turned just in time to see the hammer descend, and after that, nothing, until now. As his eyes grow more accustomed to the gloom, he is startled by the realisation that he is trapped in some kind of basement. Over in the far corner is a chair. Someone is sitting there, he realises. He strains to see. It's Caroline. Suddenly, she is speaking.

"Hi, Steve. Do you like it here? You'd better, because you're never going to leave. This is where Jenny was found. You remember Jenny, don't you? My little sister was crazy about you Steve, but you let her down and broke her heart. Do you really think you can do that to an innocent girl and get away with it? More fool you if you do. I thought about handing over her computer and her phone to the police, let them deal with you, but they wouldn't be able to pin anything on you. After all, she killed herself, but you were responsible, Steve. Anyway, it was all there on her computer: all your correspondence; the photos you sent her of yourself. Even the pathetic ad you used to entice and deceive her."

Caroline rises slowly from the seat, steps forward and produces a photograph for Steve to see. It's a picture of the gormless uncommunicative bitch; the one he dropped like a hot cake, but he didn't lead her on; Christ—he only saw her once—that was enough! She was obviously unstable; delusional; with suicidal tendencies. If only Caroline would give him the chance to explain, but it seems that Caroline has already made up her mind about him, and is intent on dishing out her own form of justice. He can see the rats now; the place is alive with them, skulking in the shadows, gearing up to feed.

HUMANITY'S NIGHTMARE

What I've come to think of as "Humanity's Nightmare" started late one afternoon as I sat in my study, struggling to complete a chapter of my latest novel. I was just about to embark on yet another minor re-write when suddenly my wife, Trudy, burst into the room looking frightened out of her wits. I stared at her nonplussed. "Hey, what's up? You look as white as a ghost."

She pointed frantically towards the window. "Look outside, Will, I swear to God, you won't believe your own eyes."

"Are you serious?"

"Just do it!"

So I did and immediately wished I hadn't, for the landscape I knew so terribly well had changed beyond recognition, comprising a dark, forlorn sky obscured in part by thick spiralling plumbs of ash cloud that completely obliterated vast areas of underlying terrain. And in the midst of all this chaos, hanging in that desolate alien sky like a dying ember, was the earth's sun, or what remained of it. I observed the spectacle in horrified fascination whilst thinking crazy thoughts of black holes and collapsing stars.

"What are we going to do?" Trudy asked as she joined me at the window.

I shrugged, at a loss to know; whilst outside the sun continued on its rapid journey into what I sensed was certain oblivion. As a result of this the landscape was losing colour and definition. It was as if some gargantuan shadow had settled over mother Earth.

"It looks diseased out there," Trudy remarked all of a sudden.

The description was, I thought, pretty apt. Ugly, distorted shadows spread across the road and filled the gardens and driveways. The shadows appeared to be three-dimensional. They moved like living entities. Of course, that was impossible, I told myself. They were just shadows.

The failing light played tricks on the eyes. Trudy, always so girlishly pretty with her flawless skin and honey blonde hair, suddenly looked older than her years. She caught me observing her, and frowned curiously.

"You're staring, Will. What's wrong?"

"Nothing," I lied.

She looked sceptical, and checked her appearance in the study mirror.

"Oh my God," she cried, "I suddenly look ten years older!"

I scrutinised my own reflection: same story.

"Are we dying, Will, is that it?"

I tried to speak in order to reassure, but words failed me.

In silence, we returned our attention to the window. Gazing out, we continued to watch with mounting trepidation as the sun and the earth appeared to perish before us.

All of a sudden, Trudy drew my attention to the computer screen. I blinked, hardly able to believe what I was seeing. The Word document I'd been working on had disappeared, replaced by an e-mail, the title of which was, "KING OF HORROR, SIMON KEANE, WANTS TO TALK."

"Do you think it's a virus?" Trudy ventured uncertainly.

"It's always a possibility." I looked back out of the window again. Things were noticeably blacker out there. And I do mean blacker! It was as if an intangible oily stain was spreading over the land. And it was getting colder. The house was starting to feel like a fridge.

"Are you going to open it?" Trudy asked, referring to the e-mail.

"Of course I am. It says it's from Simon Keane!"

"But you don't know that for sure, Will. What if opening it makes the computer crash?"

"It's a chance I'm prepared to take. Besides, there are worse things that can happen. All you've got to do is look outside to realise that."

Trudy took my point and fell silent. I clicked on the e-mail. It read, HI WILL STEPHENS. IT'S SIMON HERE, SIMON KEANE. WE NEED TO TALK URGENTLY ABOUT WHAT'S HAPPENING. I KNOW YOU'RE A BIG FAN OF MINE, AND I'M SURE YOU'LL AGREE TO HELP. WHAT DO YOU SAY? ARE YOU GAME?

I looked at Trudy, as if for guidance, when in fact I'd already made my decision. Without waiting for her to answer I clicked on the REPLY button, typed in the word, YES, and then clicked on SEND.

"Do you think this is wise?" she asked nervously. "Anybody could be hiding behind that e-mail."

I ignored her and waited. Moments later, I received another e-mail purporting to be from Simon Keane. This time, trusting my gut instinct, I opened it without hesitation. Suddenly, a series of agonised screams breached the air outside. Trudy let out a horrified gasp.

"What on earth is happening Will?"

"I-I don't know. I wish to God I did. Better make sure all the doors and windows are securely locked downstairs."

"You think someone might try to break in and hurt us?"

I thought about how the world outside our front door was changing so rapidly and so insanely, and nodded my head. My breath was vaporising, I realised. The room temperature had dipped again. I asked Trudy to go and turn the heating on. While she was out of the room, Simon Keane's second e-mail popped up on my computer.

WILL, SO GLAD YOU'VE DECIDED TO CONVERSE. WE'RE IN A TIGHT SPOT. THINGS ARE HAPPENING FAST: TOO FAST. I DON'T KNOW HOW YOU'RE COPING IN ENGLAND AT THE MOMENT, BUT OVER HERE IN THE STATES THE LONG SHADOWS HAVE ALREADY ECLIPSED MOST OF MAINE AND PARTS OF WASHINGTON STATE. CALIFORNIA IS NEXT. THEN IT'LL BE CHINA'S TURN, FOLLOWED BY INDIA. EVENTS ARE UNFOLDING JUST AS I FORETOLD IN MY NEW STORY. THIS KIND OF STUFF HAS BEEN HAPPENING ON A SMALL SCALE FOR A WHILE NOW. REALITY HAS BEEN BLURRING. PARTS OF WHAT I WRITE SEEM TO PREDICT THE FUTURE. REMEMBER THAT SHORT STORY I WROTE ABOUT THE GIRL WHO HAD THE ABILITY TO TELEPORT LIKE THEY DO ON STARTREK? WELL, I DON'T KNOW WHETHER OR NOT YOU HEARD, BUT

THERE'S A THIRTEEN-YEAR-OLD GIRL IN SANTA BARBARA WHO KEEPS DISAPPEARING AND TURNING UP IN PLACES MILES AWAY FROM HOME. SHE CAN'T EXPLAIN IT, NO ONE CAN. I WROTE THE STORY AND THEN BAM! IT HAPPENS. DID YOU READ MY STORY CALLED TWENTY THOUSAND LEAGUES AND MORE..., A SKIT ON THE OLD TV SHOW, STINGRAY, ABOUT A SUBMERSIBLE THAT SEARCHES OUT INTELLIGENT AQUATIC LIFE FORMS? GUESS WHAT: THERE REALLY IS A STINGRAY, ONLY IT'S CALLED WHITE POINTER, AND MY SPIES IN WASHINGTON DC TELL ME THAT WHITE POINTER HAS DISCOVERED ATLANTIS AND THAT THE PLACE IS INHABITED BY INTELLIGENT ALIEN BEINGS. AS YOU MAY KNOW, THAT HAPPENED IN MY STORY. I COULD GO ON BUT YOU GET THE PICTURE, I'M SURE. WELL, MY NEW STORY, "THE REALTORORS", SEEMS TO BE FOLLOWING IN THE SAME CRAZY FOOTSTEPS AS THOSE I'VE JUST MENTIONED. FICTON IS BECOMING REALITY. "THE REALTORORS" IS THE SCARIEST STORY I'VE EVER WRITTEN, WILL. AND IT SEEMS TO BE COMING TRUE BEFORE IT'S EVEN BEEN PUBLISHED! I'M CONVINCED THERE ARE REAL REALTORORS OUT THERE THAT HAVE HOMED IN AND ARE MAKING IT HAPPEN. THEY ARE DRAWING ON MY IMAGINATIVE POWERS FOR THEIR OWN ENDS. THERE'S ONLY ONE WAY TO STOP THEM FROM DESTROYING HUMANITY, AND THAT IS BY WAY OF A MAJOR RE-WRITE! WE DON'T HAVE MUCH TIME! ARE YOU STILL WITH ME, WILL, OR ARE YOU FREAKED? I REALLY WOULDN'T BLAME YOU IF YOU WERE, MY

FRIEND. AND I WOULDN'T PUT YOU THROUGH
THIS IF I THOUGHT THERE WAS AN ALTERNATIVE,
BUT THERE ISN'T ONE. YOU'RE THE ONLY PERSON
WHO CAN HELP ME, AND DARE I SAY IT, THE
WORLD AT LARGE!"

I read those final words in a state of shock and
disbelief. Simon Keane was a literary legend. He'd
ruled the supernatural horror market for the past
three decades; longer than I'd been alive! He was my
favourite author, more than that; he was my hero, to the
extent that I'd been a member of the UK arm of his fan
club for most of my adult life. As a fellow writer I could
only dream of reaching the dizzy heights he had
reached—yet for some unknown reason he had decided
I was his closest ally in what he considered to be
an imminent global catastrophe, for which he was
responsible!

I could hear Trudy moving around downstairs,
organising things, as was her way. I could imagine
her locking and bolting the doors, checking to see if the
window locks were secure, checking our food supplies,
ensuring we were prepared for all eventualities. And
while she was doing that, I sat in front of the computer
screen, debating whether or not to reply to my all-time
favourite author. Of course, there was always the
chance I was conversing by e-mail with some kind of
cyber nut case, but I didn't think so, somehow. It was in
the writing style, you see. I could tell at a glance that
Simon Keane was the author of the e-mail's I'd just read.
I was just about to start typing a reply to the revered
Mr Keane when Trudy suddenly shouted up the stairs
to me.

"Will, come quickly!"

I sprang from my seat and headed downstairs. Trudy was in the front room staring out of the window onto the road outside, the view of which was all but obliterated by the sinister encroaching blackness. I could sense movement out there nevertheless—shadowy figures skulking around. But it was the face staring back at us from the end of the drive that had prompted Trudy to beckon me, for it belonged to my father.

"Can't be," I said in a choked voice.

Trudy, who was with him the day he suffered his fatal heart attack, clutched my hand and squeezed. I blinked and the vision, if that's what it was, disappeared, swallowed by the inky blackness, from within which came more of the tormented screams we'd heard earlier. This time, they were accompanied by the sound of dogs howling and birds screeching insanely. I pulled down the blinds and turned my attention to Trudy.

She looked zoned out. I asked her if she was okay. She nodded and smiled, but the smile was unconvincing.

Back in my study, with Trudy sitting at my side, I replied to Simon Keane's latest e-mail.

SIMON: OUTSIDE IT IS TURNING PITCH BLACK. IT'S LIKE THE SUN HAS SUDDENLY DIED. I GET THE IMPRESSION THERE ARE THINGS IN THE BLACKNESS THAT ARE BETTER LEFT ALONE. WHAT EXACTLY IS IT THAT YOU HAVE WRITTEN? WHO ARE THE REALTORORS? AND WHAT MAKES YOU THINK I CAN POSSIBLY HELP?

And then I waited.

Trudy, staring out of the window, broke the silence. "It looks so horrible out there, Will. It's so desolate and depressing." She took a deep breath. "It's not like night time is it?"

I thought about lying, but couldn't. "No Trudy, it's not."

"It feels like everything is withering and dying." She looked at me, as if seeking confirmation.

I obliged with a slight nod of the head.

She turned to face the window again, seemingly drawn by the ever-thickening blackness.

Another e-mail popped up on the computer screen.

WILL, WHAT CAN I SAY? I'M A WRITER AND I WRITE. YOU KNOW HOW IT IS. YOU GET AN IDEA AND GO WITH IT. WELL, DESPITE MY DEEPENING CONCERNS ABOUT THE REALTORORS, AND AGAINST MY BETTER JUDGEMENT, I WENT WITH MY LATEST IDEA AND WROTE IT: BIG MISTAKE. I SHOULD HAVE HEEDED THE DREAMS. I REALISE NOW THAT THEY WERE WARNING SIGNS. TO ANSWER YOUR QUESTION, THE REALTORORS ARE REALITY MAKERS, AND THEY HAVE MY MEASURE. THEY HAVE SOMEHOW GOTTEN ONTO MY WAVE LENGTH. MY STORY, IRONICALLY ENTITLED THE REALTORORS IS, IT SEEMS, ABOUT TO BECOME REALITY! THE REALTORORS ENDS WITH THE DESTRUCTION OF MANKIND. AS I SAID BEFORE, THERE'S ONLY ONE WAY TO STOP THAT FROM HAPPENING. THE STORY MUST BE REWRITTEN AND IT MUST BE DONE CONVINCINGLY, AND YOU'RE THE MAN TO DO IT, WILL. NOW LISTEN CAREFULLY; THE NEXT E-MAIL YOU RECEIVE FROM ME IS GOING TO HAVE AN ATTACHMENT TITLED, THE REALTORORS. YEAH, THAT'S RIGHT; MY LATEST

NOVEL, AS YET UNPUBLISHED, WHICH YOU ARE GOING TO READ, EDIT, REWRITE WHERE NECESSARY AND END IN A COMPLETELY DIFFERENT WAY. GOT IT, WILL? I AM EFFECTIVELY ASKING YOU TO REWRITE A PRE-ORDAINED FUTURE! NO MEAN FEAT MY FRIEND.

I had a question, a seemingly obvious one, which read: SIMON, WHY CAN'T YOU SIMPLY REWRITE THE STORY YOURSELF?

BECAUSE, he quickly replied, AT THE BEGINNING OF THE REALTORORS, THE MAIN CHARACTER, WHO HAPPENS TO BE THE AUTHOR OF THE STORY IN WHICH HE IS DEPICTED, IS GOING INSANE. GET IT? I WON'T BE SOUND ENOUGH OF MIND TO REWRITE THE GODDAMN STORY EVEN IF I WANTED TO! IT'S ALL IN THE STYLE AND THE IMAGINATION, WILL. I THINK YOU HAVE IT IN YOU TO DO IT, TO FOOL THE REALTORORS! SO HERE GOES KID. LOOKSIE HERE, WE HAVE AN ATTACHMENT. I HOPE YOU CAN SPEED READ AND TYPE DEFTLY BECAUSE THERE REALLY ISN'T MUCH TIME. NO PRESSURE THEN. I CAN FEEL MY MIND FLOUNDERING, WILL. I PROMISE TO STAY AROUND AS LONG AS I CAN BUT DON'T BE SURPRISED IF THE E-MAILS SUDDENLY TURN TO GOBBLEDEEGOOK, OR CEASE ENTIRELY. AT THAT POINT YOU'LL BE ON YOUR OWN. BEST OF LUCK, KID AND MAY THE FORCE BE WITH YOU—HA, HA!

Were it not for the desolate landscape confronting me on the other side of the window pane, I may well have dismissed the e-mail as some kind of crazy joke, but the terrifying scene outside was irrefutably real.

Trudy suddenly announced she would check the news channels for reports on what was happening. In the meantime I replied to Simon Keane's latest e-mail, using two simple words: WHY ME?

A minute or so later, I got a response.

FOR ONE, I FEEL I CAN TRUST YOU, WILL. YOU'VE BEEN A LOYAL SUPPORTER OF MINE AND YOU ALSO HAPPEN TO BE A DAMN GOOD WRITER! YOU MAY BE SHOCKED TO LEARN THAT I HAVE READ YOUR WORK, AND ALTHOUGH MY INFLUENCE IS VERY APPARENT IN YOUR STORIES, THEY ARE NEVERTHELESS ORIGINAL AND WORTHY OF MERIT. THE INFLUENCE BIT IS IMPORTANT, HOWEVER. THE REALTORORS MUSTN'T KNOW IT'S NOT ME DOING THE REWRITE. IF THEY DO, THE REWRITE WILL BE IMPOTENT, AND THE GAME IS UP FOR GOOD.

All of a sudden, Trudy called up to me.

"Will, come downstairs; check this out!"

I joined her just in time to witness a television report declaring that the country was now in a state of emergency. Riots had broken out in many towns and cities and a major earthquake had rocked the capital, where hundreds were feared dead or injured. An incident, an explosion of some kind, had occurred in Wales which had razed most of Cardiff to the ground. A huge fissure had split the earth wide open where the M6 joined the M42, and sea levels on the east coast had risen by three feet in the past two hours, causing widespread regional flooding.

"Things are happening out there that defy belief!" was how one anxious commentator put it, while a studio-based reporter hinted that the blackness overtaking England and other parts of the world contained hidden dangers not yet fully understood. Any film footage was of inferior quality due to poor visibility, but it was nevertheless clear that the army had been brought in to help the police contain trouble and restore calm.

Trudy and I stared disbelievingly.

"Come on," I said, switching the television off, "let's get back upstairs. We've got work to do!"

"You go," she told me firmly. "I'll stay down here; make sure we don't get any unwelcome guests." With that she disappeared into the kitchen, returning moments later brandishing a huge chopping knife.

I stared in amazement. "You'd really use that?"

"If I have to..."

Simon Keane's as yet unpublished manuscript was roughly seventy thousand words long, a pretty short effort by his standards. It began like most of his stories, with everything appearing to be normal, at least on the surface, before gradually descending into a monstrous literary abyss. I didn't bother printing the manuscript but read it straight off the screen. I was a man in a hurry. Even then I felt time was slipping by with increasing rapidity; like it was quite literally speeding up and running out. As for Simon Keane's story, as usual there came a point when it lost its ordinariness, and turned that fear-inducing corner into nightmare alley.

Just as that happened, there was an almighty bang against the window pane. I reeled back in my chair, automatically covering my face with my hands, expecting glass to shower me, but it didn't happen. The force of the projectile, whatever it was, lacked the necessary power to do lasting damage. I rose gingerly from my chair, put my face close to the window pane and looked down. Due to the strange oily blackness invading the landscape it was hard to see anything at all by now, so I couldn't be entirely sure what I was seeing down there: a large bird perhaps, or some kind of gigantic insect. Whatever it was, it was big with a bulbous head and membranous wings; and it was unmoving, which is how I hoped it would stay.

Trudy's voice pulled me back to reality.

"What was that noise, Will?"

"Just a bird," I said thinking quickly. "It must have lost its bearings due to the blackness."

She stood in the doorway, looking frail and scared, and much older than her years. She continued to hold the knife like it was her best friend, whilst gazing at me curiously, as if she suspected I was lying to her.

"Are you all right babe?"

She nodded stiffly; then headed back downstairs where she made a series of phone calls to friends and relatives.

Meanwhile, I continued to read. At some point I noticed that the time given on the computer screen said 4:41p.m. GMT. I was sure it had said 4:05p.m. GMT the last time I had looked a couple of minutes ago. I checked my wristwatch for confirmation. My watch told me it was 4:47p.m. GMT.

I called out to Trudy: "What time do you make it?"

"5:05p.m.!"

"What does the clock on the mantel say?"

A slight pause, and then: "This is crazy, Will: it says it's 5:20p.m.! What's going on?"

"There are those who believe time to be an illusion," I called back. "Perhaps they're finally being proven right." A thought suddenly struck me. I checked the time on the computer screen again. It showed 5:35p.m. Twenty-five minutes had passed in the blink of an eye. Suddenly it hit me; the reason Trudy and I appeared to be ageing was that time was speeding up! The world was hurtling towards total oblivion! Reality itself was in the process of changing! The dead were rising! The Apocalypse was dawning! I had to get moving with the re-write, and fast!

I don't know how long it took me to complete the first part of the task. It appeared events had blown the natural time continuum to smithereens, but when I did arrive at that point, I suddenly realised I was pretty much clueless on the subject of how to rewrite what in effect was the ultimate literary version of Armageddon! I just kept thinking, oh my God, Simon, what have you gone and done, over and over. The guy really had outdone himself. The story was absolutely terrifying! It also left me with a terrible dilemma. You see, Simon Keane's story ended with humanity being wiped off the face of the earth. I suddenly got to wondering whether that would be such a bad thing. Humanity had, after all, got an awful lot to answer for. Why not just sit back and let Simon Keane's story reach its natural conclusion without interference? It might well be for the best. With humanity gone, mother Earth would no doubt prosper. I made my thoughts known to Trudy. She went ballistic.

"What the hell's the matter with you, Will? Humanity's on the brink of extinction and you turn into a crazy idealist! You'll be handing the world's population a death sentence if you choose to go down that road! How can you even contemplate such a thing?" I opened my mouth to speak, but she cut me off. "Why can't you simply write an ending that sees humanity saved from itself, and the earth miraculously cleansed of all the crap that we've dumped on it?"

I tried to explain that it didn't work like that, but Trudy refused to listen and stormed out of the room shaking her head in frustration, still holding the chopping knife. It seemed that I was on my own. The big question was: did I save the human race or destroy it and leave in its wake a better, cleaner and more peaceful world? Talk about playing God. I had to consider something else too, something extremely important: my re-write of Simon Keane's story had to keep ahead of real life events for obvious reasons. I therefore had to begin at a point I felt wouldn't be overtaken by those events. Trouble was, the later in the story I left it to start the re-write, the more momentum real life events would have gained. Seemed I had the mother of all deadlines to contend with.

Outside, a creature the size of a light aircraft majestically crossed the blackened horizon, before soaring high above a burning warehouse to disappear into the ether. I followed its progress in stunned disbelief. Other alien life forms appeared out of the blackness, in the form of thick slime ridden tentacles that suddenly dropped from the skies to strike out at anything that moved. What in Christ's name had Simon Keane unleashed with his latest horror story? But that wasn't the worst of it. In the time it had taken me to read Simon's story, activity outside had seriously picked up pace. There had been a lot of shouting and screaming, distant explosions, and gunshots. I'd even heard the sound of helicopters flying somewhere overheard. And it was all taking place in a surreal inky blackness.

Electricity was the only thing keeping us from falling into a totally sightless existence. The way things were heading, I guessed it was only a matter of time before the electricity did fail, and we lost not only the lights, but the power to the computers and everything else that functions by means of that particular energy source. How in God's name would I save the world if that happened, Simon Keane? The thought brought the apparent craziness of the situation home to me and I almost laughed aloud. Will Stephens, saviour of the universe! I really couldn't see it myself.

Trudy re-entered the study, still clutching her new found pal, the chopping knife. Shockingly, she had aged years in the ten minutes or so since I'd last seen her. From the look she gave me, I guessed it was the same story with me.

"Have you finished reading yet?" she asked, sidestepping the issue.

I nodded.

"And what's your conclusion?"

"Don't ask. Who have you been calling?"

"Anybody and everybody: it's total chaos out there. Nobody knows what's going on." She nodded towards the computer screen. "Looks like you've got your work cut out, Will. Best I leave you to it."

She came over, kissed me lightly on the forehead, and then left. I immediately hunkered down at the keyboard, fingers poised, but nothing happened. I had a sudden case of writer's block. I couldn't decide which of my two storylines I should go with.

In the end the decision was made for me. Trudy spotted a child wandering around outside: a little boy, three or four at most, crying out in obvious distress. I guess her maternal instincts must have kicked in. With no thought for her own safety and unbeknown to me, she left the house to go to the child's aid. The first I knew about it was when I heard her scream and looked through the study window to witness one of the monstrous tentacles lay claim to her. She vanished in a puff of red black smoke. The little kid ran off, screaming like a banshee.

For what seemed like, and probably was, an extremely long time, I was unable to function, while outside the horrors borne of Simon Keane's imagination continued to plague humanity.

And then, seemingly out of nowhere, came the all inspiring light bulb moment, which allowed me to put aside my grief and think once more about writing. And that's exactly what I did. I wrote for my life—for everybody's life, if Simon Keane was to be believed.

As for the new ending, it saw the Realtorors fall victim to the Earth's contaminated atmosphere. I kind of liked the irony, and dare say Trudy would've too, had she still been around.

As soon as I was finished, I e-mailed Simon, with the message, JOB DONE: WHAT NOW, and silently prayed for a lucid reply. It came soon enough and read as follows:

SEND IT, BUDDY, SEND IT, RIGHT NOW! IT'S NO GOOD UNLESS IT REPLACES THE ORIGINAL MANUSCRIPT. AND FOR THAT TO HAPPEN IT HAS TO BE ON MY HARD DRIVE. FINGERS CROSSED THE REALTORORS DON'T REACH THE END OF THE STORY BEFORE THAT HAPPENS. SO LIKE I SAID, GET IT OVER ASAP! OH, I NEARLY FORGOT; ONCE YOU'VE SENT THE MANUSCRIPT TO ME, ENSURE YOU DELETE

ALL CORRESPONDENCE BETWEEN US. THEN DESTROY YOUR COMPUTER.

I e-mailed back: ARE YOU MAD?!

He ignored the question simply saying, PLEASE, WILL, JUST DO AS I SAY. IT'S OUR ONLY CHANCE!

So I did as he asked. I sent the rewritten version of his story, deleted all of our correspondence to date, and then I waited for a reply or at the very least, a read receipt.

Neither arrived.

I e-mailed Simon again: ARE YOU THERE?

Nothing; sweet FA.

I glanced through the window. Outside, hundreds of the revolting giant tentacles dangled from a black, tormented sky in search of victims. In the street below, figures ran around in utter confusion. There was a lot of screaming and angry shouting. A man inadvertently brushed against one of the slug-like tentacles, screamed madly and went up in a cloud of dark red smoke, just as Trudy had.

It took five more e-mails to Simon before I finally got a reply.

It simply said: THANKS FOR THE STORY, DUDE!

I e-mailed him straight back with: HAVE YOU READ IT?

His reply went: NO LONGER HAVE THE NECESSARY CONCENTRATION; BESIDES, NO POINT. IT'LL EITHER WORK, OR IT WON'T. HERE'S LOOKING AT YOU KID! SIMON.

P.S. DON'T FORGET TO DELETE EVERYTHING AND SMASH YOUR COMPUTER!

I took a deep breath; then did as instructed. It almost broke my heart to do it, for there was a lot of personal stuff on that machine—letters, stories, photos of Trudy—but somehow I managed it, emptying the hard drive of every single piece of information it contained, before finally destroying the computer itself with a lump hammer I found in the garage. That done, I sat and waited. I'd done everything I'd been asked to do. Man's destiny was now in the lap of the gods, or should that be "laptop" of the gods?

I guess I knew the light-bulb moment had worked when I heard movement on the landing outside my study. I was gazing through the window, observing the blackened sky slowly brighten as sunlight fought its way back into reality, when Trudy entered the room. It'd been her selfless act with the child that had ultimately decided me on which storyline to choose. I suppose you could say she had restored my faith in human nature; made me think that yes, maybe there was hope for humanity after all. As for Trudy's subsequent death and resurrection, well, there was nothing in the rules that said a little artistic licence couldn't be employed in the rewrite of Simon Keane's nightmarish story. The brief was credibility, no more and no less. Besides, she was a minor character who wasn't even given a mention in Simon's version of events. No one would ever be any the wiser, certainly not the Realtorors.

There was one slight problem, however: in my haste to incorporate her reincarnated self into the rewrite of Simon's story, I'd neglected to describe her as she was prior to her death, so what I got back was the version that had perished in the lethal grip of the giant tentacle. The red cloud of smoke that signalled her demise was, I now realised, a sudden explosion of blood! She kind of went "pop!" I'll be honest; when I saw the state she was in, the first thought that entered my head was, *rewrite!* Trouble was, the manuscript was already submitted. Rewriting reality was no longer an option.

LOATHE THY NEIGHBOUR

It's Sunday morning, and Ronald Billington-Smythe, retired civil servant and self appointed president of the local neighbourhood watch committee, storms into his picture perfect living room seething with rage and indignation.

"I just don't believe it," he growls with sinister intent, "the blithering idiot is at it again!"

"What was that, Ronald, dear?" asks Pearl, Ronald's long-suffering wife

"Big ears: he's drilling or tile cutting or some such thing! I'm going to box those humungous ears of his to a pulp if he's not careful. You just see if I don't, bloody DIY idiot!"

"Please, Ronnie," Pearl says in an attempt to mollify, "he's only doing a spot of home improvement."

"Home improvement: I'll give him home improvement!"

Bill Broadbent, Ronald and Pearl's new neighbour, is outside on his driveway sawing a piece of wood for the new rabbit hutch he is making for Bill Junior, when Ronald emerges from the house, ready for battle.

Bill looks up from where he is working, sees Ronald and smiles amiably.

"Good morning, lovely day!" he says in greeting.

"I've got a bone to pick with you," says Ronald, straight to the point.

"A bone," Bill repeats, frowning.

"Yes, a bone, there's no other way to say it. You're disturbing us and it just won't do. We're quiet-living people, Pearl and I, and we've a right to quiet enjoyment of our property. I think you'll find it states that quite clearly in the title deeds and it's no use saying otherwise."

Ronald is suddenly interrupted by his little terrier dog, Jasper, who darts between his legs yapping for all he is worth. Ronald commands the dog to be quiet, but as usual it ignores him.

Bill Broadbent, meanwhile, has come to stand on the other side of the privet hedge that separates his driveway from Ronald's. The sudden confrontation has caused his face and ears to turn bright red.

"Now listen here," he starts, trying to be heard above Jasper's persistent yapping. "All I'm doing is a bit of pottering around. I'm making a rabbit hutch for my son. Is that really such a major crime?"

"Perhaps not," Ronald grudgingly agrees, "But I'm concerned it might be a case of little acorns turning into giant oaks. Last week you were tile cutting."

"For my kitchen" Bill explains reasonably.

"Noisy," insists Ronald, "Very noisy indeed. Pearl was trying to nap. Even with ear plugs, and Pachelbel's Canon playing in the background, it was impossible: the week before it was hammering all day and into the early evening. It sounded like our house was about to fall down around our ears. Whoops, sorry!"

"You exaggerate, surely?"

"Are you calling me a liar? Jasper, do be quiet. Well, are you?"

"You're putting words into my mouth," says Bill, rapidly losing patience.

"Words into your mouth," Ronald repeats indignantly, "Now listen here: I expect an improvement in your behaviour, Mr..."

"Bill, call me Bill."

"I'd rather not, if you don't mind. As I was saying before I was so rudely interrupted: I expect a little consideration, if not for me, then for my wife. Pearl suffers migraines. She's under the doctor for them, you know. She was hospitalised with one once: very nasty it was too. The doctors were really quite concerned; thought it might be a tumour."

"I'm sorry to hear it."

"There's no need for sarcasm."

"I wasn't being sarcastic!"

"Anyway, I've nothing against a neighbour improving his property. All I ask is that it is done quietly, and with the minimum of fuss."

"Have you quite finished?" Bill asks, whilst tapping the saw against the side of his leg in a considering manner.

"For the moment." Ronald pulls himself up to his full height of five foot two and turns to go.

"Stop right where you are!" Bill commands in a low but firm voice.

Ronald freezes on the spot, while Jasper runs around in circles yapping dementedly.

"You've got a nerve," says Bill, ears flushed red with suppressed fury. "My God, criticising me when you open and close your garage door all day and all night!"

"Our tumble dryer resides in there," Ronald explains.

"And your stupid little dog," Bill continues unabashed, "yaps its brainless head off from dawn till dusk and you have the audacity to dictate to me about what I can and can't do on my own property! Ye Gods! Give me strength!"

"I'll give you a thick ear if you're not careful."

"You and whose army?"

"Like that, is it," says Ronald digging his hands into his trouser pockets, nervously jangling loose change. "If that's your attitude young man, you leave me with no choice but to contact my friends at the local council. Let them decide the rights and wrongs of this sorry affair!"

"Don't you think you're over reacting?" asks Bill, still trying to come to terms with the sudden turn of events.

"Over-reacting!" cries Ronald, "First you accuse me of being a liar and then of being a neurotic. How dare you!"

"That's not what I meant and you damn well know it!" Bill retorts.

"Don't you get abusive with me," Ronald growls, waving a plump forefinger, "or I'll have the police on you!"

"Go on then, make the call," Bill says nonchalantly. "See if I care."

Ronald glowers at the younger man. "Don't you worry, I will. You've upset the wrong person here. I have contacts and influence in this town."

With that, Ronald storms back into the house with Jasper yapping close on his heels.

"Goodness me, Ronnie," Pearl chides as he steps into the front hall, quivering with rage. "You're going to have to calm down or you'll give yourself a heart attack. And did you really have to confront our new neighbour like that? He seems like such a nice young man."

"He started it!" Ronald exclaims, eyes bulging insanely. "Anyway, whose side are you on?"

Pearl, ringing her hands nervously, wary of her husband's quick temper, stammers, "W-Why, yours of course."

"It doesn't sound like it from where I'm standing." Ronald jabs a short fat thumb back over his shoulder. "Our new neighbour, as you so kindly refer to big ears, is an absolute nightmare. He just won't listen to reason! Well, he's picked on the wrong man with me, Pearl, wouldn't you agree?"

Pearl stares apprehensively. "What are you going to do, Ronnie?" she asks, recalling the string of unfortunate incidents involving past neighbours who failed to comply with her husband's strict code of conduct concerning neighbourhood relations. There was Mrs Jenkins, whose tabby cat insisted on fouling Ronald's flower bed. In the end, the tabby disappeared under mysterious circumstances, never to be seen again.

Then there was the Carmichael family. Mr Carmichael upset Ronald by repeatedly parking his car across their drive, by only a few inches, but it was enough. Mr Carmichael's car suddenly began to suffer mechanical problems, culminating in brake failure, which almost cost him his life.

And then there was Mrs O'Leary, whose pet budgie upset Ronald with its constant chirping. The budgie, fondly referred to as Bertie by Mrs O'Leary, disappeared from its cage one day, having been placed on the back patio to enjoy the summer sun. Pearl was convinced that but for her constant intervention over the years, other troublesome incidents would surely have occurred. It seemed that she was forever trying to talk her hot-tempered husband out of getting back at those who inadvertently upset him. She often likened living with Ronald to living with a small, vindictive child.

"One more squeak out of him," Ronald is saying as Pearl looks anxiously on, "and he's for the high jump... you mark my words, my sweet."

Pearl, filled with deep concern for their new neighbour, watches immobilised, as her husband waddles into the sitting room, quietly humming the theme tune to Rocky.

One month and numerous confrontations later, Ronald sits in the kitchen reading the morning newspaper, quietly chuckling to himself. Pearl regards him warily out of the corner of her eye, wandering why he is in a good mood all of a sudden. Last week saw him and Bill Broadbent almost come to blows over Bill's DIY antics. It had been a close call, thought Pearl. Ronald later told her that he would have pole-axed the man he'd taken to calling "odd job" in preference to "big ears" had he not been struck down with a sudden case of severe indigestion.

He hadn't let it rest all week. Then, for no apparent reason, he'd stopped complaining to her about "odd job", which was a concern, as this behavioural pattern had occurred before in her husband, just before Mrs Jenkins tabby cat went AWOL; just before Mr Carmichael nearly carped it due to his car's brake failure, and just prior to Bertie the budgie's sudden vanishing act. She couldn't help thinking that some kind of mishap was certain to befall their new neighbour and his family.

Then, one day there's a knock at the front door. Pearl answers it to find Bill Broadbent standing there.

"I'm sorry to bother you," says Bill, smiling politely, "but I don't suppose you've seen Thumper on your travels?"

Pearl frowns in ignorance. "Thumper...?"

"My son's pet rabbit; he seems to have disappeared from his hutch. Last night he somehow managed to slip the catch and escape."

Pearl gulps back a sense of deep apprehension, recalling that at some point during the early hours Ronald had left the marital bed, complaining he was unable to sleep and was going for a walk.

"I can't help you, I'm afraid," she tells Bill as calmly as she can. "If I do see Thumper, I promise you'll be the first to know."

Bill thanks her and goes away, scratching his head in bemusement. The following day finds Ronald and Bill at loggerheads again, this time over Bill's decision to replace the privet hedge dividing their driveway with a dwarf wall.

"You can't do it!" Ronald erupts, his podgy face the colour of beetroot. "I simply will not allow it!"

"Oh, but I can," says Bill; "and I will. If you care to check the boundary plans to our respective properties, you'll see that this hedge belongs to me!"

Incensed, Ronald momentarily forgets himself. "Now listen here, big ears..."

"What did you call me?"

"Big ears," Ronald repeats unapologetically, "or would you prefer odd job? Oh, and by the way, how's Humper?"

"I think you mean Thumper," Bill corrects, "and if I discover you're responsible for Thumper's disappearance, I'll have you hung, drawn and quartered!"

"We'll see about that," Ronald says defiantly, before quickly retreating to the safety of his house.

The next morning, there is a rap at the door. Ronald answers it to find Bill standing there, holding a letter.

"My son received this in the post today," says Bill, watching carefully for Ronald's reaction. "It's from his pet rabbit who says he has left us, never to return."

"And what's that got to do with me?" Ronald asks warily.

"He must've forgotten how to spell his name," says Bill through narrowed eyes. "He's signed himself off as "Humper". Wasn't that the name you used when referring to him?"

"Go away," Ronald says, slamming the door shut.

But Bill isn't finished. "Return the rabbit or face the consequences!" he rants through the glass pane now separating them. "I know you've got him! Do you hear me, you odious little man, return Thumper or else!"

"Get lost!' says Ronald from behind the coat stand, "I never even laid a hand on your stupid rabbit!"

That evening Ronald leaves the house to partake of his routine constitutional with Jasper, but for some reason fails to return.

"Where is your master?" Pearl inquires of Jasper, having answered the dog's anxious pawing at the front door. Jasper, normally so vocal, fails to raise so much as a whimper on this occasion.

"Oh dear," says Pearl, considering the implications of what has happened, for she has already noted the mysterious excavation work that has suddenly taken place in Bill Broadbent's back garden, noted also the hefty timber crate that occupies the ground nearby, a scene which Pearl can't help likening to that of a coffin lying beside an open grave.

That night, Pearl retires to bed full of sudden optimism for the future. A feeling that is further fuelled by the fact that next morning the excavation in Bill

Broadbent's back garden is neatly filled in, with the timber crate nowhere to be seen.

"Like your new vegetable patch," says Pearl when she next bumps into Bill.

Bill thanks her, whilst attempting to beat a hasty retreat. Pearl, who is like a woman reborn, stops him firmly in his tracks.

"Not so fast, young man. I think you and I have some serious talking to do."

Bill's face drains of colour. "Talking, what kind of talking?"

"For a start," says Pearl, appearing to relish the moment, "my front door requires a lick of paint, and the side gate needs a drop of oil. Think you can help?"

"Of course," Bill obliges, whilst looking mightily relieved. "Isn't that what neighbours are for?"

LOST AND FOUND

Sandra's on tenterhooks: 8:30p.m. and John still isn't home, and not a word from him to explain why. It goes against the grain. John is annoyingly steadfast, predictable to a fault. You could set your watch by his movements. Up at 6:00a.m. every weekday morning come rain or shine, 8:00a.m. on weekends and holidays, a quick jog round the block, no more than a mile, then breakfast - porridge and toast, black coffee, one sugar. Even sex has to be time-tabled: twice a week, on Friday and Sunday, same old routine for everything. That's John, and it's a part of the reason Sandra loves him. Boring to some he might be, but he's reliable, the ultimate "Mr Dependable", and for Sandra, that's what counts most. There are never any surprises with John; even his name sounds boring, but one thing's for sure, he will never, ever let you down. Home by 6:00p.m. every evening for the past six years except for one occasion when he broke down on the motorway, but she got a phone call to say so: so her mind was put at rest. So where is he? What has happened to him? There was no answer from his office earlier, or from his mobile. Broken down again maybe, even though the car is brand new, part of his promotion package. Yeah, that's it, thinks Sandra, he's broken down in an area where he's unable to get a phone signal.

And then, just when she's ready to think the worst and contact the police, the landline phone out in the hall rings out. She rushes to answer it.

Breathless, she snatches up the handset.

"Hello, is that you, John?

Silence: she happens to glance up at the clock on the wall, which tells her it's 4:09p.m., wrong time, the clock has stopped. Beneath the digital readout giving the time is another which gives the date. 09.09.09. All the nines, she thinks vaguely.

"Hello? Who's there? Speak to me."

Nothing.

Crank—it must be a crank, she thinks angrily. She's just about to slam down the phone when quite suddenly and without warning a voice filters through from the other end of the line. It's faint, distorted, virtually drowned out by white noise in part, but it is there, a background sound, and it is John speaking.

"Sandra," he says, straining to be heard, "help me!"

Sandra's heart races; she feels suddenly faint, nauseous. She's about to speak, to ask her husband what the hell is going on, but is distracted by her young daughter, Ellie, who toddles out into the hall holding a pencil in one podgy hand, and a drawing pad in the other.

"Mummy..."

"Not now, darling," says Sandra, the phone handset pressed tight to her ear, "mummy's busy. I'll be with you in a moment."

"Will you draw me a picture?" asks Ellie, hopefully.

"After I've finished on the phone," promises Sandra. Ellie seems to consider this as if it is of major importance, before finally turning and wandering back into the kitchen.

"John," Sandra says anxiously into the phone's mouthpiece once she's gone, "what on earth has happened?"

"Help me," he says again through the static that threatens to engulf his voice, "I've made a terrible mistake sweetheart; I've put myself in a bad place. I didn't think it would be like this. I thought it was the answer to my problems..."

"What are you talking about John? You're not making any sense."

"I don't have much time," he says in a faint, echoing voice. "If I don't get back before they find me, I'm done for. Maybe it's already too late for me."

Breakdown, Sandra thinks, he's had a damn breakdown. Working too hard, that's what it is, the new position is too much for him. She's been telling him to slow down ever since he won the promotion six months ago. The job is too high-powered, too demanding; he's obviously found it difficult to cope, and finally collapsed under the stress.

"Christ, this is terrible," John says suddenly.

"What is?" Sandra asks, feeling helpless, whilst gripping the handset so tightly, her knuckles have turned white.

"I panicked," John blurts out. "She said she would destroy me."

"Who did? You're not making any sense."

"If she contacts you, ignore her."

"Who? Who are you talking about?"

"Alex..."

"Who the hell is Alex?"

"I'm so sorry," John says. "It's getting dark in here, and your voice is growing faint. I feel like I'm fading..."

Sandra, distraught now, with tears rolling down her cheeks, says, "Please John, explain. Where are you? Who is Alex?"

The line goes dead.

"Mummy, why are you crying?"

Sandra turns to see Ellie observing her from the kitchen doorway. She fights to compose herself. It's hard, but she manages it, just.

"I'm all right honey," she assures the four-year-old. "Mummy's just being silly."

"Where's daddy?"

"Working late, he'll be home soon."

Ellie wanders off. Once she's gone, Sandra contacts the emergency services and experiences a mixture of disappointment and mild relief when she discovers that no one of John's name and description has been admitted to either of the two hospitals serving the area. The police, for their part, can offer little in the way of advice or support.

"If your husband hasn't made contact within another forty-eight hours call back and we'll issue a missing persons report," says the duty officer she speaks to.

Come the following morning, with Ellie at day nursery, Sandra receives an unexpected visitor.

"Hi, my name is Alex," says the pretty blonde she finds standing on the doorstep when she answers the door. Alarm bells start to ring, although Sandra cannot quite believe what she is thinking. John, an adulterer? How absurd!

"My husband has mentioned you," Sandra says, whilst trying to make sense of the situation. The woman called Alex looks surprised. "He has?"

"Yes, he has. Do you know where he is?"

"At work, I would imagine."

"He didn't come home last night. Needless to say, I'm worried sick."

Alex shows no reaction, so Sandra, standing to one side, continues: "You may as well come in. I trust this won't take long."

"No, it won't take long at all," Alex tells her.

They enter the living room. "Please, take a seat," says Sandra.

"Thank you," Alex replies and chooses a seat by the window. She really is quite stunning, Sandra thinks to herself as she takes the seat opposite: mid-twenties, slim, leggy, with flawless skin and baby blue eyes. Sandra swallows back her mounting apprehension and prays that Alex isn't here to deliver a bombshell by announcing that she is John's secret lover. Sandra wants to laugh aloud at the thought; how ludicrous, she thinks. John simply wouldn't know where to begin—he's too shy for a start: definitely not a lady's man. Why, it had taken him forever to ask her out on a first date, even though she'd made no secret of the fact that she liked him.

"So, what's this about?" asks Sandra, not really wanting to know, afraid despite herself, that the gorgeous young woman sitting in her living room is about to shatter her safe little world.

A faint smile touches Alex's perfectly formed lips as she says, "Hasn't John told you? I did think that by your reaction, he had told you already."

Sandra frowns, and shakes her head in ignorance. Suddenly, she feels sick to her stomach. It seems that her gut instinct might be correct.

"Told me what?" she asks apprehensively.

Alex's smile broadens imperceptibly, "About us of course."

"A-As I said before," Sandra says choosing to ignore the remark, whilst fighting to retain her composure. "I haven't seen or spoken to my husband since early yesterday morning. He didn't come home last night. I've been going out of my mind with worry. What's happened to him? If you know, you must tell me."

Alex ignores the question and gazes around the room, taking in her surroundings for the first time. "You have a nice house, Mrs Smith," she says finally. "You must be very happy living here."

"Who exactly are you?" Sandra asks, rapidly losing patience with the stranger. "How do you know my husband? Who is he to you? Tell me right now, or leave!"

Alex, crossing her perfectly formed legs, replies, "I wanted to meet you, I needed to know what's so special about you that when it came to the crunch, he was prepared to forsake me for you. He must really love you, Mrs Smith; that's all I can say."

Sandra, still in denial, says, "I-I don't understand," when in reality she understands perfectly. Alex is indeed her husband's secret lover. But that's not all as it turns out and when Alex speaks next, Sandra feels as if a knife has been plunged into her heart.

"I'm pregnant with your husband's child, Mrs Smith. And do you know what his reaction was when I gave him the news?"

Sandra stares at the young woman, unable to comprehend what she is being told. Her head is buzzing with confusion; tears of anger and frustration are coursing down her face, her lips are trembling—in fact her whole body is shaking.

"He began to cry," Alex tells her with obvious disdain. "He thought he could have his cake and eat it.

A typical man—I stupidly thought he was different, that he was kind, considerate and dependable, someone I could trust. I knew he was married, of course. He didn't try to deceive me, I'll give him that, but he said his marriage was all but over, that you and he had grown apart, that he was bored with you and with your marriage, and I fell for it hook, line and sinker."

"Bored with me," Sandra repeats numbly, the irony only too evident.

"I told him he must take responsibility," Alex continues, "that he can't just walk away from a situation of his own making, but he didn't want to know. He told me," and for the first time a flicker of emotion touches Alex's doll-like features, possibly conveying her own feelings of frustration and confusion. Her sparkling blue eyes cloud over. She bites her lip as if a brief stab of pain will somehow lessen the emotional turmoil within. "He told me to get rid of it; said he'd pay, how generous, and tried to buy me off. As far as he was concerned, I was suddenly just the little office floozy, the dumb blonde who's outlived her usefulness and had to be gotten rid of. He showed his true colours Mrs Smith—proved to me he's a charlatan and a low life. Nevertheless, I wanted him, still want him to do the right thing and own up to his responsibilities. It isn't right that he can behave like he has and think he can simply walk away; there's a price to be paid Mrs Smith. It takes two as they say."

"I-I don't know where he is," Sandra says distractedly, too stunned to think clearly. She opens her mouth to say something else, but nothing will come. She has stopped shaking. She sits perfectly still, unable to move. Her feelings and thoughts are in complete disarray. She feels suddenly dead inside. This was the reason John hadn't come home last night. He was scared and had taken the coward's way out. He'd phoned her, possibly with the intention of admitting his guilt, but had bottled it. Coward, he was a coward, as well as an adulterer. Sandra, staring at the floor looks up to see that Alex no longer occupies the seat by the window. She looks round. The young woman now stands by the door that leads out into the hall, apparently making ready to leave, no doubt happy to have got the whole sordid business off her perfectly formed chest.

"Is that it?" Sandra says, standing. "Is that all you've come to say?"

Alex frowns curiously (even with a frown on her face, she looks stunning, thinks Sandra) and says, "What else is there to say, Mrs Smith?"

"What else is there to say?" Sandra repeats contemptuously, "How about sorry? How about telling me how sorry you are for ruining my marriage, and my life, you little bitch!"

But Alex has already left the room. Before Sandra has time to react, the front door is heard to open and slam shut, and a deathly silence descends upon the house. A moment later the silence is replaced by the sound of Sandra's uncontrollable sobs.

Later, just before Sandra leaves the house to collect Ellie from day nursery, the phone rings. In her rush to answer it, Sandra slips and falls heavily onto the ceramic tiled floor, banging her head in the process. There is blood, not much, just enough to leave a faint red smudge on a single white tile. Sandra, groggy and nauseous with pain, manages to stand and get over to the phone before it stops ringing. She snatches up the handset with a shaky hand and speaks into the mouthpiece, saying the first thing that comes into her head.

"John, is that you?" As she says this, she happens to glance up at the digital clock hanging on the wall, which tells her it is 4:09p.m. on 09.09.09, just as it did the previous night when John had phoned.

"John," she says again when she fails to receive a response from the caller. "Speak to me, I know it's you. Please say something, anything."

A moment later she gets her wish. "I'm sorry," John says in a faint, hollow sounding voice. It sounds to Sandra as if he's speaking from somewhere deep inside a cave.

"Is that all you have to say?" she says, barely able to contain her anger. "Do you really think that is all it takes to make things right between us—a pathetic apology made in a phone call? Alex told me all about it in case you're wondering; all the sordid details. How could you?! Eleven happy years, or were they? Bored, she claimed you told her you were bored with me, and our marriage. That's rich, coming from you. Dull but dependable, was how I always thought of you. How wrong can one person be about another?"

"Sandra, listen to me," John says desperately, "I've made a terrible mistake."

"Too damn right you have," Sandra interrupts.

"I panicked when Alex threatened to spill the beans. I can remember exactly how I felt—sick and desperate. I saw no way out. It seemed such an almighty mess. I was going to lose everything: you, Ellie, the house—my life, in fact, because you and Ellie *are* my life."

Sandra, her head fuzzy from the fall she took; slumps down onto the seat by the hall table. Her husband's voice, she thinks—something just isn't right with it, or was it her imagination? Had the fall somehow affected her hearing? She squeezes her eyes shut tight in an attempt to clear her aching head.

"I got in my car," John was saying, in that weird-sounding far away voice, "and I drove around for a while, not knowing what to do. Eventually, however, I reached a decision. So I filled the car up with petrol, Sandra, I got a good length of hose and a roll of gaffer tape from a plumber's merchants, and then I went and bought a bottle of Scotch. After I did that, I had a bit of a cry. Then I drove up to the Ridge. Remember the Ridge, Sandra?"

Sandra, fighting back tears of anger and sadness, manages a weak "yes", whilst thinking back to when they'd gone to that out crop of land as young lovers, when they'd first started dating.

"Yes, I remember," she says and feels fresh tears come.

"Last thing I recall is glancing at the dashboard," John says, "and noticing the date - 09.09.09: all the nines. I thought about calling you but it was four in the afternoon, you would've been out of the house collecting Ellie. Doubt I could've summoned up the courage anyway. When I came round the first thing I did was look at the dash and saw it was still 4:09p.m. on 09.09.09, only it was dark, so I guessed the electrics must be playing up. At that point I reached another decision, and tried to start the car, but it was no go, the damn thing was out of fuel. Then I started to remember, and realised why. That's when I really started to panic and I phoned you."

A lengthy pause followed, throughout which Sandra sat rigid in her seat whilst gripping the phone handset as if her life depended upon it.

"I have to get back before they find me, Sandra," John says, breaking the uneasy silence. "I think that if

I can get back before they find me, it'll be all right. They don't know what's happened; no one does, so the way I look at it, I can turn back the clock, in a manner of speaking. But once they find me, it's over."

"John, who are you talking about?" Sandra asks. "You're not making yourself clear."

"My question to you is," John says, ignoring her, "Is it worth my while coming back—can you forgive me and allow us to sort this mess out? I need to know, Sandra, it's important. Life is meaningless without you and Ellie. I've been a fool, I know it. If I find a way back, Sandra, will you let me in?"

Sandra, shaking uncontrollably, with tears streaming down her face, sighs despairingly. "No John, I'm sorry, I can't."

"I understand," John replies resignedly. His voice, already faint, starts to recede until it is barely audible. "So let them find me. Getting back was probably wishful thinking anyway. Tell 'em where I am, Sandra. When they do eventually discover me, they'll come knocking to give you the bad news. You'll be sad despite it all, but you'll get over it. I love you Sandra. Remember that, and I'm truly sorry."

And then, quite suddenly, the line goes dead.

Glancing up at the digital clock hanging on the wall, Sandra, completely drained through emotional upset, sees it is 3:15p.m. on 10.09.09. She wipes her eyes and stands, shakily, thinking of Ellie all of a sudden—she must get going or she will be late to collect Ellie. Any thoughts of John can wait until later, after "they come knocking", as he'd put it, to confirm the awful truth to her.

MEECES TO PIECES

Harold Bishop is sitting quietly in the front room of his modest suburban semi, when all of a sudden, his Sunday afternoon piece is shattered by an ear piercing scream. It comes from the bathroom where his wife Hilda, is taking a bath.

Harold immediately drops the paper he is reading, rises from his seat as quickly as his sixteen-stone frame will allow, and hurries to his wife's aid. When he arrives on the landing huffing and puffing, he finds Hilda standing in the bathroom doorway dripping wet, with a fluffy pink towel wrapped around her ample body.

"It's that ruddy mouse again," she declares angrily, from beneath a mop of the gingeriest hair imaginable. "It waited until I was half out of the bath and at my most vulnerable, then pounced!"

"Hilda," Harold says with forced patience, whilst resting a chunky hand against the banister, "mice may do a lot of things, but I can assure you that pouncing on people is not one of them."

Hilda is unconvinced. "How else would you describe it, Harold? I tell you, it lay in wait until I was half in and half out of the bath, and then shot straight out of the shadows and ran across my bare foot with the speed of a runaway train!" Hilda shudders at the memory, before tip-toeing across the landing into the bedroom. Harold watches her go, likening her gait to that of a rather dainty pink hippo.

"Get rid of that mouse, Harold!" she says, poised to slam the door shut. "It's like having an odious non-paying lodger! Get it Harold. Seek and destroy!"

"Seek and destroy," Harold repeats despairingly. "What *does* she think I am—an Exocet missile?"

Returning to the comfort of his old stuffed chair, a wedding present some thirty-five years ago, Harold ponders what to do about the mouse problem. It's one that's been with them on and off for weeks, if not months. Baited traps haven't worked; poison hasn't worked. Close surveillance and covert operations haven't worked. The only option left appears to be to call in the professionals, but that costs money and Harold has an aversion to spending money. Maybe he should get rid of Hilda, he thinks whimsically; surely mice would be easier to live with. They certainly wouldn't eat or spend as much! They wouldn't nag, either.

In bed that night, Hilda, in curlers and a thick flannelette nightdress, suddenly plonks her Mills and Boon novel down on her lap, turns to Harold and says, "Well, have you had any ideas?"

Harold, lying flat on his back snoring heavily, is shocked awake from the most wonderful dream in which he is stranded on a desert island with Cheryl Cole, to find Cheryl's angelic face replaced by Hilda's stern ginger features.

"What was that dearest? Ideas, what kind of ideas? I'm really not sure I'm fully awake."

"Oh do shut up, Harold, you blithering idiot. I asked you if you'd had any ideas about how to get rid of our little squatter?"

Harold thinks frantically, but nothing comes to mind. "Maybe they'll go away of their own accord," he ventures lamely.

Hilda looks at him sharply. "So you think there's more than one, do you?"

"That's not what I said, Hilda."

"You said "they"; I heard you distinctly."

"A figure of speech, that's all."

Hilda scowls and returns to her book. And that's how things are left. Until, that is, the mouse problem rears its ugly head again some days later. This time Hilda is positive she hears them (she is convinced there is a plague of the little critters since Harold made his off-guard remark), scurrying around in the loft, and sends Harold up there to investigate.

"There's nothing up here but junk and cobwebs," he says peering down at her through the hatch.

"Are you absolutely sure, Harold?"

"Positive. Well, as positive as I can be without clearing everything out of here."

"Then perhaps that's what you should do," Hilda suggests.

"But it'll take me forever."

"It'll give you something useful to do now that you're retired. It'll give your life purpose!"

Reluctantly, Harold returns to the task at hand and spends the next hour up in the loft searching for the illusive intruder, or intruders.

He reaches the far side and suddenly the light goes out. The loft is plunged into darkness. On all fours, he looks around blindly, before crawling slowly back to the open hatch.

"Nothing," he tells Hilda on entering the kitchen where she is busily washing up the dirty dishes.

"Useless," comes the reply.

"I tried my best," says Harold despondently.

"Well plainly your best is not good enough, Harold Bishop. We have mice infesting the house and they must be evicted."

The next day while Hilda is in town doing the weekly shop, Harold decides to take a nap in the bedroom instead of getting down to the list of odd jobs Hilda has left for him to do. While the cat's away, Harold thinks with an impish little grin, and makes himself comfortable on the bed while formulating an excuse in his mind to explain why he has neglected the allocated jobs. Tummy ache, that'll do. "Sorry Hilda, I was just about to re-inspect the loft for the mouse, (he is always careful nowadays to use the singular when talking about their little problem), when all of a sudden, I got a terrible case of stomach cramps and had to come for a lie down." Yep, that'll do nicely.

In a matter of minutes, Harold is in a deep relaxing sleep. When he awakes, having sensed movement on his chest, he is shocked to see he has a visitor in the shape of a small white mouse. It sits on his chest, gazing down at him through a pair of the pinkest and meanest eyes he has ever seen. Whiskers twitch frantically as the mouse says, "Listen carefully to me, Harold. My name is Michael, Mike to my friends," he gives a quick backward nod of the head and Harold realises with amazement there are more mice peering at him from the vantage point of his oversized gut, "and I have a proposal for you. Keep me and my friends in cheese and we'll take care of your problem."

Harold stares in shocked disbelief. "W-What did you say?"

"You heard," says the mouse belligerently, "Cheese in exchange for evicting the ginger nut."

"B-But she's not my problem, you are," Harold argues.

"Who says?" asks the mouse.

"Hilda of course."

"She would say that, wouldn't she?"

"I-I don't understand."

"She's using us to throw you off the scent. She's your problem, not us! We're here to fix it for you, Hal. It's a once in a lifetime opportunity. What do you say: cheese in exchange for a peaceful life?"

Harold, afraid to move for fear of dislodging his visitors, has a long hard think. Hilda's demise in return for a few chunks of Stilton: what could be simpler? The offer is tempting, more than tempting, Harold decides—it is thrilling!

"Done!"

Michael winks a beady pink eye at Harold and says, "You won't be sorry, Hal."

Harold, warming more and more to the idea, agrees, "She's the bane of my life, Mike. Get rid. You have my blessing."

Next day, while Harold is in the garden tending to his tomatoes, a sudden high pitched scream comes from inside the house, followed by a short series of loud thuds, and then silence. Upon entering the front hall, Harold finds Hilda lying flat on her back at the foot of the stairs with her head at a peculiar angle. Plainly, she is no more.

"Happy now?" a voice asks from the top of the stairs.

Harold looks up to see Michael gazing down at him, surrounded by all his rodent pals. There follows much excited squeaking and scurrying, which in turn excites Harold, who claps his hands together with glee. "Happy? I'm bloody ecstatic! As for you meeces, I love you to pieces!"

Michael rolls his little pink eyes heavenward. "Cut the sentiment, Hal, all we want is the cheese. We expect a daily delivery, made up of the finest cheeses money can buy."

Harold frowns worriedly. "For how long?" he asks, concerned about the financial cost of such an agreement.

Michael blinks. "How long is a piece of string, my fat little friend?"

"I thought we were talking about a one off-payment," Harold complains, "What you're suggesting will work out extremely expensive for me!"

Michael is unimpressed. "The ginger one was insured, wasn't she?"

"That's not the point."

"Cut the crap, Hal. Make sure the first delivery is available for us tomorrow morning. And make sure there's plenty for everyone!"

"But I have to see to Hilda first," says Harold, glancing down at her stricken body. "There are people to see, arrangements to make."

Michael remains unsympathetic. "Show us the cheese Hal, or you go the same way as your fellow porker!"

"But I need time, Mickey," Harold pleads miserably.

"The name is Mike," the mouse corrects. "Mickey is a stupid cartoon character. Remember, Hal, first thing tomorrow."

One night not long after Hilda's funeral, Harold is woken by the sound of purring in his ear. He turns on the bedside lamp and is amazed to see a fat ginger cat sitting next to him on the bed.

"You finally went and did it, didn't you, Harold?" says the cat peevishly. "I knew you had it in for me, but I never thought you would ever have the courage to go through with it. Was I really that bad?"

Harold stares agog. "Hilda, is that you?"

"You've got yourself in a fine pickle this time, haven't you, Harold? Good job I'm back, so I can take care of you, great lump of lard that you are. But a word of warning: if you want me to tear Mad Mick and all the other meeces, to pieces, payment will be an ongoing supply of the very best fish known to man. In fact, I'll expect the very best of everything, and that includes milk and cream! Is that understood?"

Harold has a quick think. The title Mad Mick is more than apt for Michael. Since Hilda's demise, he and his band of scurrying reprobates have almost bankrupted Harold with their extreme demands. Cheese flown in from abroad on a weekly basis has almost laid the coffers bare. Living with Hilda had been challenging, but it was nothing to sharing your home with a psycho mouse and his cronies!

"Nice to have you back," Harold tells the cat, meaning it.

"Nice to be back," says the cat with a great big Cheshire grin.

ONE-EYED JACK

I was with Sam, my partner of over three years, when it happened. We were on holiday hiking along Finley Gorge, having set off earlier that day from a local B & B following a night spent socialising with the locals. It had ended up being a late one, so we were both suffering, but like I said, we were on holiday, so minor over indulgences were allowed. Initially, the weather that day was a mixed bag, but we were hopeful it would at least hold out until we'd completed the walk.

"What do you think you'll do, Joe? Sam asked me as we negotiated a steady incline towards a monolithic structure rising from the terrain's summit. I glanced over at her, not quite understanding, my hangover still evident, blurring my thinking processes.

"About your job, dummy," she elaborated for my benefit. "It's been your only topic of conversation for the past couple of weeks."

"Oh, that," I said, mulling the question over as if for the first time. "Dunno. We need the money, so I guess I'll have to put up and shut up, but I really don't know what I'll do when it comes right down to it."

"A case of I used to think I was indecisive but now I'm not so sure," Sam teased. I glanced at her, unsure whether the comment was spoken with humour or mild irritation. It'd become harder to read each other since Sam had dropped her little bombshell.

"I'd leave if I could," I said almost to myself. "I hate the ruddy job."

"I hate my job," Sam replied.

"Then I suppose it becomes a matter of degree," I reasoned.

"Or perhaps," Sam said, "Some of us are made of sterner stuff."

I glanced at her once again, but was unable to gauge her thoughts. Was she joking or was she mildly contemptuous of me? I didn't know, not anymore. We were like strangers compared with how we'd been up until a few weeks ago. Sam, her profile lost beneath the broad hood of her anorak, gave what sounded to me like a despairing sigh.

I gently nudged her. "Come on, I'll race you!" I said, hoping the challenge might alleviate the tension that had developed between us.

"Okay," she agreed, "but no cheating."

"As if!"

We ran along a shingle path that curved down towards the forest edge. Then we were crossing a bridge that spanned a fast-flowing brook. The bridge led us into an area of grassland.

We'd managed maybe a couple of hundred yards when Sam suddenly slipped and lost her footing on the damp ground. She let out a yelp of pain and fell to one knee. She was holding her ankle when I reached her.

"Are you okay, Sam?"

She looked up at me grimacing. "Don't ask stupid questions—of course I'm not."

I squatted down beside her. "Do you think you can walk?"

She slowly stood, flexed the injured ankle, and took a couple of tentative steps forward. "I think I'll live," she said, wincing slightly, "But it's sore, Joe. I don't think I'll be racing you again today."

I retrieved the guide-book from my coat pocket. It informed me that the walk we'd elected to do was nine miles long, would take a reasonably fit person approximately four hours to complete, and was classified as "medium to difficult". Sam and I had done a fair amount of hill walking in the time we'd known each other, so we'd been pretty confident about undertaking this particular walk. Until now, that is.

I looked up to be confronted by an overcast sky. Dark, heavy rainclouds loomed threateningly in the distance. We might be in trouble here, I thought. My wristwatch stated it was a little after one thirty in the afternoon. The partying episode with the locals meant we were late setting off that morning. Following breakfast, Sam and I had returned to our room where we'd both fallen back to sleep. By the time we'd finally got going, it was almost midday. We weren't even at the halfway stage at the point where Sam had twisted her ankle, but the option of retracing our steps was a non-starter. The first part of the hike was easily the most difficult, with an extremely steep incline to navigate that overlooked a deep ravine. The pathway, I recalled, had been alarmingly narrow and hazardous. It was one Sam would have a major problem re-negotiating. We had no alternative but to keep going. Hopefully, we'd complete the walk before daylight faded, or the weather took a turn for the worse, if of course, Sam's ankle was up to the job.

I estimated we had just over two hours of daylight remaining. Enough time for an uninjured person maybe, but we were no longer in that category. It was November—come four p.m., it would be virtually dark. I looked further up the track. Ahead loomed a towering monolith, beyond which more dark sinister clouds gathered. And as I stared forlornly at the monolith and the clouds, it began to spit rain. Nothing major; just mizzle, but it was cold and would undoubtedly get colder still as the day progressed.

Sam was speaking, I realised. "Let's just hope and pray "One-Eyed Jack" doesn't put in an unexpected appearance."

I frowned momentarily before remembering. Last night, at the bar, one of the locals had tried to spook us with the tale of a man nicknamed "One-Eyed Jack", who'd started a house fire in an attempt to kill himself and his family—motive unknown.

"He hadn't long returned from fighting in the Great War," the storyteller had explained. "He'd fought in the trenches. Unhinged him by all accounts, like a lot of others who'd been involved in fighting for King and country. Mind you, Jack Briggs, to give "One-Eyed Jack" his real name, was never ever going to go to Heaven. He was a law breaker before he went off to war and he fell back into his bad old ways as soon as he was demobbed. Getting drunk, fighting, burglarising the community, terrorising those who dared try to stand up to him. He was a rum un, all right. Survived the fire, he did, which is more than could be said for his wife and child, but lost his face to the flames, together with the sight in one eye."

"What happened to him?" Sam had asked, quietly intrigued by the tale.

"Just before he was supposed to go to trial," said the storyteller, "he escaped from his prison cell and fled to the moors, never to be seen again. Local folklore insists he perished there, and that his spirit haunts the area."

"It's cold," Sam remarked as we crossed a heathery plateau.

"And it's going to get colder," I replied as I took in the chill, barren landscape.

We trudged on a little further, in virtual silence. We were perhaps three or four hundred yards from the monolith now, which marked the half way point of our trek. I checked my watch again. Nearly two o'clock.

"Can't you walk any faster?" I asked Sam. She was trailing me, limping slightly: right ankle. I saw her wince and suck in breath.

"You're in pain, aren't you?" I observed.

"I'm fine," she answered gamely.

"What will we do if you suddenly can't walk?" I asked, voicing my fears.

She ignored me.

I gazed around, surveying the surrounding terrain. The immediate area was completely flat, wide open to the elements. I searched for a building of some description but there wasn't one to be seen.

"Christ..."

"What did you say?"

I turned. Sam trailed me by maybe five yards or so. She was struggling and falling behind.

"Nothing," I said, "just thinking aloud."

"You might have to carry me," she said, as she hobbled closer.

I looked in shocked surprise: "Four and a half miles!"

"Piggyback ride then." She smiled wanly. "Don't worry," she continued for my benefit, "It's not that bad." She frowned. "Not yet, anyway."

By now, the light drizzle had turned to rain, and I was regretting the fact that we'd ever come to this neck of the woods. Yet at the time, a hiking holiday had seemed to be the answer to our problems. Heaven knows, we both needed a break of some kind. It'd been a bad year for us. In January, I was made redundant. Things got tight. We panicked, sold the house and moved into rented. I finally got back into work in September but hated the job from day one. The hours were too long, the money was crap and the stress was immense. As if that wasn't bad enough, Sam suddenly announced she intended leaving me due to my unreasonable behaviour. I begged her to give me one last chance.

"I've never laid a hand on you," I'd said in my defence, "never so much as threatened you."

"You don't understand," she'd replied. "Your mood swings are the problem, Joe. If you don't get your own way you sulk and clam up—it's awful. Worse are the looks you give me whenever I upset you, like you want to kill me. Maybe it would be better if you did threaten or hit me—at least then the aggression would be out in the open. You bottle things up, Joe. I worry that one day, I'll do or say the wrong thing, and you'll explode and something really bad will happen."

Despite her misgivings, Sam agreed to grant me my wish and give me one last chance. So there we were, halfway through a walk that had seen the weather deteriorate alarmingly, and Sam become lame, for God's sake. And if that wasn't bad enough, neither of us could get a signal on our mobiles.

"Joe?"

"Huh?"

"Are you okay?"

"As well as can be expected given the circumstances. Why do you ask?"

"You were staring at me."

"You used to like me staring at you."

Sam was silent, and looked blankly at the ground. I looked past her, back the way we'd come, to a point where a fence was interrupted by a rickety stile. A figure was approaching from the other side. I should have been pleased, given our circumstances, but for some reason, I wasn't. Whoever it was staggered as if drunk, and from what I could see, was inappropriately dressed for the great outdoors.

"Come on, let's go," I said returning my attention to Sam. "We need to get a move on. Weather's closing in. It'll be dark before we know it."

Sam started over to me, the limp more evident, her expression noticeably strained. By now, the rain was coming down in thick, ice-cold sheets. The ground was sodden and slippery. The situation was becoming dire. We both knew it, and feared for the consequences.

Finally, we made it to the monolithic structure, which was in fact a war memorial that commemorated those servicemen who had given their lives in the Great War. It stood approximately twenty feet high, with a steep, stepped base. Countless names were engraved into its marble surface. I thought about "One Eyed Jack", who had survived the nightmare scenario of that war only to succumb to a further nightmare of his own making. Why'd you do it Jack, I found myself wondering, why'd you kill your wife and kid? What did they do to you that was so bad? Were they about to abandon you? Was that it? Had your wife found someone else whilst you were away fighting for King and country? Was that the reason for the sudden act of madness?

I glanced over at Sam, who was busy studying the endless rows of names decorating the monolith, seemingly oblivious to my presence. Don't ever leave me, Sam, I thought as I turned to face the incline we'd just ascended. In the middle distance, having crossed the stile, was the shambling figure I'd spied earlier. Whoever it was, was heading in our direction.

"Are you ready to carry on?" I asked Sam, who had sunk down onto the base of the memorial in order to take the weight off her feet. She looked up at me from beneath her soaking wet hood and frowned in deliberation before finally nodding. I went over to her, my intention being to help her up.

"Leave me alone, I'm perfectly all right," she said tetchily. She managed to struggle to her feet unaided, looked at me and slowly shook her head.

"What's wrong now?" I asked her.

"What's wrong?" she repeated in an ironic tone. "My God, Joe, look at us, look where we are! Look at the state of me. I can barely walk. My ankle is killing me, and I'm scared we won't make it back before the weather and the dark gets us. People have died out here, Joe. All we've got to keep us going is bottled water and the remainder of a stupid packed lunch. And you ask me what's wrong!"

I took a tentative step towards her. "Come on, babe, it's not that bad. We'll be back at the inn before we know it, you just see if we're not. You can have a nice warm bath and rest up."

A sudden gust of wind whipped around the monolith as I said this. Leaves and debris scattered like confetti. Sam shuddered beneath her coat and looked to be on the verge of tears.

"Why do I always listen to you, Joe?" she asked in a trembling voice. "We move to the other side of the country so you can take a job that you're destined to lose in the blink of an eye. You make us buy a house we can't afford, and you recommend a holiday that could get us hospitalised or worse! Why on earth do I ever listen to you?" She was becoming hysterical. I reached out to take her in my arms but she pushed me away.

"You always think a hug will make everything right between us, don't you, Joe. Well, it won't." She glanced around frantically, eyes narrowed against the unrelenting wind and rain, as if searching for a means of escape from the terrible situation we found ourselves in. Finally, she turned to me, saying, "Get me out of here, Joe—right now!"

Her contempt for me was obvious. As far as she was concerned, I had failed her. I tried to speak, but could think of nothing to say, probably because there was nothing *to* say. A quick glance back over my shoulder and I spotted the stranger once again, continuing to narrow the distance between us.

Turning back to Sam, I said, "You haven't changed your mind about us, have you?"

Without answering, she hobbled off, having to brace herself against the elements. I caught up with her and we walked in silence for a short distance—until that is, she suddenly announced that she had changed her mind about us staying together.

"It's not going to work," she said tearfully. "It's over, Joe. Can't you see that?"

I grabbed her by the arm and spun her to face me: "You can't leave," I remonstrated. "I won't allow you to!"

But it was already too late. The stranger saw to that. He came out of nowhere, and suddenly Sam was screaming: screaming for dear life...

And that is the last thing I remember, up until the time the questioning, the accusations and the denials began.

SNUGGLE

I get home, exhausted, and go straight into the kitchen where I make myself a cup of tea. I take the tea into the front room, where I notice an empty glass. I don't remember it being there when I left for work that morning, although I could be mistaken. I don't like things lying around making the place look untidy, so before I settle down with my freshly brewed cup of tea, I take the glass into the kitchen, and stand it neatly on the drainer. Having drunk the tea, I head up to the study where I intend to start an assignment for work. Life revolves around work nowadays—there doesn't seem much else to do.

As I cross the landing I pass by the master bedroom. I don't sleep in there anymore. Too many memories. The door stands ajar. I can see inside. The bed is unmade, but how's that possible, I ask myself.

When I left for work this morning, it was made; I know it was made, because that's how it was when I got the call, and it hasn't been slept in since.

I go into the study, where I switch on the computer and check my emails. And as I'm doing that, I happen to glance over at the window, where a picture of Julia stands. Brown hair, brown eyes and lightly tanned skin—gorgeous...

I set to work, typing, fingers moving deftly over the keyboard—until that is, I spot Julia's rings and bracelet peeking at me from behind the computer. I have to physically touch them in order to convince myself they're real. They shouldn't be here; they've been consigned to the loft, in a little wooden box, under lock and key.

How long now? How long since she went away? Two weeks: three, maybe? I check the calendar on the desk, and realise it's been longer than I thought: time has got away from me. Tomorrow, it will be one month to the day. An anniversary, of sorts...

I continue working until late. I don't even have an evening meal or any supper; just work. Julia always said I worked too hard, but I can't help it. I get it from my father. I've got worse since it happened. Twenty-nine, heart attack, gone, just like that.

It's almost midnight: time for bed. I have an important meeting to attend in the morning, in the city centre, not to be missed.

I glance around. I can see into the master bedroom from where I sit. Standing on the bedside table is a coffee cup. She was always leaving things lying around. It was one of her idiosyncrasies.

Tonight, for the first time in a month, I decide to sleep in the marital bed. The sheets are crumpled, in disarray, as though someone has slept there recently; as though someone sleeps there still. The sheets are warm, or is it my imagination?

In bed, I imagine her lying beside me, just like the good old days.

"Snuggle," I whisper as I close my eyes and start to drift.

DEADBEATS

Emma, she's giving me that look again. I don't like it, just like I don't like what's happened to my home town, and beyond.

"Are you okay, Em?"

She nods her head and smiles but she's still giving me that look. I have to watch her nowadays, just like she has to watch me. Despite the fact that we love each other as much as ever, we could be seriously bad for each other's health since the so-called "change" took place.

Things started to go haywire around this neck of the woods about three months ago. A local newspaper broke the news initially, the product of a rumour that circulated around the ASMAN laboratory that stood on the edge of the Barrow Franklin Lake on the outskirts of town. No one knew exactly what went on at that laboratory, (still don't if the truth be known), other than it carried out government funded work to do with something called "universal crop protection". The source that gave the newspaper the story of an experiment known simply as ZQ42—said that ZQ42 was in reality a flying insect that had been created to protect crops from pests. Those in the know had, the source went on, proclaimed it would turn out to be the ultimate guardian of crops worldwide, and would almost singlehandedly stamp out world famine.

There was, however, a problem, added the source, which had only come to light very recently. ZQ42 was also a danger to humans. We weren't told how, just that the world at large would find out soon enough with humanity being changed forever. The source ended his or her tale in sinister fashion by saying that they were living proof of it.

At the time no one knew whether the article was a hoax, or whether it was supposed to be taken seriously. It was one of those stories that, having read it, you checked the date to make sure it wasn't April 1$^{st.}$ I took the stand that, hoax or not, the newspaper ran the story mainly because it got the imagination and conversation going.

You see, the ASMAN lab was extremely unpopular hereabouts. The local community had opposed it ever being built, and condemned it as an eyesore when it was. And everyone around these parts, without exception, hated the wall of secrecy that surrounded the place. In its time, it had been accused of all manner of things, from using animals inhumanly for experimentation purposes, to being a facility producing biological weapons, to playing God in genetics.

One month later, the story of the little critter named ZQ42 was virtually forgotten. A few weeks after that, everything started to change around here. People started going AWOL. They didn't show up for work, or they failed to return home. I own, or rather, I owned a delivery business: around that time one of my drivers failed to turn in for work. Dan Meakin, known him most of my life, a family man who's never had a sick day whilst in my employ, and that's been four years or more. Emma and I know his wife, June: we talked to her at the time, and she said she noted nothing odd in Dan's manner prior to his disappearance other than he seemed preoccupied. But she thought it was down to his mother falling ill, and that he was worried.

Dan wasn't the first to disappear, and he certainly wasn't the last. Jake, our teenage son went walkabout the following week, without so much as a by your leave. Then it was our turn to flee into the wilderness. When normality is blown out of the water, people tend to panic and run for cover, and that's exactly what's happened. People like us, the ones who have been directly affected by recent events, simply ran, knowing that to stay would invite confrontation.

As I sit writing this in a back office that was once a busy council building, but which is now a stricken empty shell with busted windows and ruined furniture, Emma, or "Em" for short, my wife and good friend of almost twenty years, squats in one corner of the room, observing me closely. Occasionally, I myself waver from the task of getting all that's happened down for posterity, and regard her with similar intensity. We both of us no doubt have the same thing on our mind.

Food.

It's a frightening thing to say, but I suspect it is only mutual love and affection that stops us from going at each other like a couple of crazed wildcats. And it's all down to our little friend ZQ42. You see, the story given to the local rag wasn't a hoax, it was horribly true. ZQ42 was indeed dangerous to humans. And then some!

A member of the ZQ42 family presently resides on the desk at which I type. It is about the size of a housefly and dark crimson in colour, which means it's recently fed, unlike Emma and I, who have survived on liquids since we fell foul to the malaise the creature inflicts on humans. Just how long our willpower will hold out for is anyone's guess, but undoubtedly there will come a time when one or both of us succumbs, just as others before us have.

At least the blood red fly resting on the desk can't hurt us anymore.

"Doug?"

It's Emma.

"What is it, hon?"

She rises slowly to her feet.

"I think I hear something, Doug."

I let my hands slide off the keyboard and I listen. She's right. Movement: coming from across the corridor. My immediate thought is, is it "Deadbeat" or "Normal" out there? That's how humanity's divided up nowadays. Racial, gender and political divides have disappeared. They no longer matter. Humanity now finds itself segregated into two distinct groups: "Normal" and "Deadbeat".

Personally speaking, I'm not altogether sure which one I fear more. Both equally, I guess, but in different ways. If it's a "Normal", he or she will be in certain peril if they dare enter the little sanctuary Emma and I have created for ourselves. The little red monster sitting on the desk will see to that. The "Normal" won't even know about it until it's too late and the change occurs. Even if he or she is wearing the protective suit that's been hastily designed in the wake of the emergence of ZQ42, there's a risk they'll fall victim to its lethal bite. You thought mosquitoes were bad. I'll tell you, brother, you ain't seen nothing until you've seen what a member of the ZQ42 family can do.

I was taking a bath when I realised I'd been had. Or should I say, the fact was confirmed to me. I'd spotted the bite mark on my arm already, purple, about the size of a shirt button, but tried to tell myself it was nothing, just a normal insect bite, like you do. It had nagged at me nevertheless, more so when I spotted a similar bite mark on Emma's neck soon after. When it happened and the so-called "change" overtook me, it was incredibly quick. One moment I was normal, the next I was "Deadbeat". I was lying there, soaking, contemplating my navel, when I decided to sink down in the bath and submerge my head beneath the soapy water, as is my habit. And there I lay for the best part of thirty seconds or so, listening to the rhythmic beat of my heart echo softly in my ears. B-boom - b-boom - b-boom...

Thirty seconds, or there a-bouts, when quite suddenly and without any warning whatsoever, the sound stopped. My heart stopped. It was as simple and as final, and as horrifying as that. I'd experienced the sound of the "deadbeat".

You might think I'd have panicked, but I didn't. In fact, I didn't even raise my head out of the water. Instead I continued to lie there, listening, hoping the scenario would change and the comforting sound of my life-giving heart would return to fill my water-logged ears again, but it didn't happen. There was no sound, nothing. Dead quiet, you could say.

Eventually, after maybe a further two minutes, I managed to rouse myself from my shocked state and sat up. I checked my wrist for a pulse, hoping against hope that it had been some terrible mistake on my part, but there was no mistake, because there was no sign of a pulse. I placed a tentative hand to my chest. No trace of a beat. Yet I continued to breathe and function quite normally.

There'd been rumours in the past few days of people "changing" in their droves: rumours also of the terrifying consequences of such a change, what it does to a person physically and mentally.

"Doug."

It's Emma again: she's staring apprehensively towards the door through which we entered this room some hours ago. In one pale hand she holds an extremely long hunting knife pillaged from one of many vandalised stores in town. I suspect she's reached the point where she'll use the thing, too.

Hunger, especially the kind we're both experiencing, is a tremendous motivator. Doesn't matter if it's a "Normal" or a "Deadbeat" out there in the corridor; *meat is meat.* Emma licks her lips in anticipation. She tenses and moves silently towards the door. I'm getting a very real sense that the famine we've both experienced recently is about to end. I sit and watch immobilised with a mixture of fear and great apprehension and, it has to be said, profound excitement, as Emma positions herself to one side of the doorway with the knife raised, ready to strike.

I want to tell her no, it's wrong, immoral, to feed off our own kind, but I can't, because I know all too well that if we are to survive (whatever that means), we must succumb: any other food source is of no use to us now. We tried it initially and experienced the side effects: unimaginable sickness, terrifying hallucinations, worse than death itself, and I guess we are pretty well qualified to know. You see, victims of ZQ42 don't actually die from the malaise the creatures of that particular family inflict, but neither do they survive. They change: not dead exactly, but neither are they alive in the true sense of the word.

We didn't want it to come to this, Emma and me. We're religious people, strong in faith, we've always believed in the principles set down in the Good Book. Live a good life, do your best, treat others how you'd like to be treated yourself, don't lie, cheat, murder, and in obeying those sacred rules, upon your death you'll be rewarded and be allowed through the gates of Heaven to meet your Maker.

Only reality, it seems, is different for us: despite our best efforts we've become entities that exist somewhere between life and death. Maybe this is purgatory that Emma and I and people like us are experiencing. Or maybe this is the dawn of Armageddon.

One thing is for sure, Emma has reached a decision: whoever is about to pass through the doorway won't get the chance to become one of us if they're not already. Emma's going to get to our uninvited guest before our little red friend has a chance to get so much as airborne.

So I'm watching both her and the empty doorway very closely, waiting expectantly for the mystery victim to enter the room, when all of a sudden something is thrown through that doorway which I initially mistake for a cricket or tennis ball, but which turns out to be a hand grenade. It flies past Emma, crossing the room at speed before rebounding off the wall opposite. From there, it rolls across the floor before finally coming to rest near a drinks machine.

We both see it for what it is now and glance at each other in abject horror. "Deadbeats" we might be, but the thought of being blown to smithereens is terrifying nevertheless. A split second later and there's an almighty explosion. For what seems like a very long time, everything goes black. When I come to, I'm lying stricken on the floor on the other side of the room from the laptop I've been recording this sorry episode on. Incredibly, the laptop remains where it was prior to the explosion, completely intact.

I narrow my eyes as I try to seek Emma out through the dust and gloom, but she's nowhere to be seen. I lay there for a few moments in shocked contemplation. I know who's responsible for the grenade attack: it's the "Normals"; they're on the offensive, trying their best to hunt down and somehow rid the world of us "Deadbeats". They see it as an "us or them" situation of mega proportions and they're right to. "Normal's" and "Deadbeats" don't mix well.

Satisfied I know who the culprit is, I check myself for injuries. It's bad. And yet, despite it all, I'm able to view my situation in a detached, objective manner, and maybe that's just as well.

Prior to the explosion I was whole-bodied, "un-dead", it has to be said, but whole-bodied. Now, however, the situation has changed markedly. No longer able to walk, I drag myself over to the far end of the room to find Emma slumped against the wall. Her predicament mirrors my own. We both took the full force of the explosion, and have paid the price. We regard each other for the longest time, finding it virtually impossible to come to terms with what has happened.

"We're damned aren't we?" Emma says finally, and I have to agree—it certainly looks that way. How it will all end is anyone's guess. Maybe starvation will get us, or perhaps it'll be the dogs that have taken to roaming the streets of late. Or maybe it'll never end. Maybe this is how it's going to be forever.

THE OTHER SIDE OF
THE TRACKS

"I've got a good feeling about tonight," says Marilyn as she lights a cigarette and blows smoke. "What about you, Eddie? Have you got a good feeling?"

Eddie smiles and nods his head, "Sure have, babe. It'll be the best ever. We're all heroes in one another's eyes, so it's gotta work. By the way, have you seen Bud? Do you think he'll show up?"

Marilyn glances over towards the door through which she entered moments before. "Don't worry, he'll be here." She takes a seat at the table and gestures for Eddie to join her. As he does so, Eddie acknowledges a second woman present.

"How're you feeling, Jan?"

"I'm okay," the woman says.

He doesn't believe her. She looks completely used up.

"Nervous? Are you nervous?"

She nods and smiles wanly.

"Like you used to be when you were about to take to the stage?"

"Yeah, but in a different way."

Marilyn nods understandingly. "I know exactly what you mean, Jan. I feel the same. I got real bad nerves whenever I performed: didn't matter what medium it was, stage, TV, film, I was always as sick as a dog before I went on. It made me late quite often. Fellow artists thought I was being prissy, being a prima donna or just plain lazy, but it wasn't the case. The truth is, I was busy throwing up. But this is easy by comparison: we got nothing to lose and everything to gain. And it'll be fun, and that's something none of us get a lot of nowadays."

"You can say that again," Jan says, rolling her eyes.

"Nerves never really got to me," Eddie tells the two women. "A rush of excitement was all I ever experienced. Call me superficial, but for me, it was like hooking up with the most beautiful gal in the world, or driving the fastest automobile ever designed."

Marilyn glances over at the door again. "Do you think the others will show tonight?"

Eddie shrugs. "Who knows? The message has gone out, so all we can do now is wait and see. Glen will, I'm sure. He's keen as mustard. He almost feels it's his duty."

"What about Jimmy?" Jan asks. "I like Jimmy. He's got attitude."

"Shame what happened to him," Eddie muses. "Kinda lost his head."

"That's sick," says Jan, meaning it.

"You're right," Eddie agrees.

"He was a real speed freak," Marilyn reflects.

"And he had the means to live his dream," Jan chips in.

"All of us did," says Eddie, reminiscing, "Unfortunately, some of us pushed it too far."

Marilyn sighs, "A case of too much too young I guess." She looks at Jan who nods and sighs.

Eddie raises his arm to check his wristwatch and then lowers it again. "Why do I always do that," he says as if to himself. "I know darned well it'll give exactly the same time as it always does. Damn thing stopped ages ago."

"How long?" Marilyn asks. "Do you know?"

"When it happened, I guess."

"Same for me," Jan remarks.

Marilyn nods agreement. "Mine still says 3:45a.m. Pretty poignant, huh?"

Just then the door opens and in walks a handsome man of middle years. He has dark hair and wears tinted spectacles. The others present regard him with a mixture of surprise and suppressed delight.

"I didn't think you'd come," Marilyn says as he joins her at the table.

"Thought I'd give it a go after all," he replies in a heavy Southern drawl. "I've been chewing over what you said the other day, Marilyn, about us owing something to all our friends back home. So I thought I'd give it a shot."

"A wise move," Eddie acknowledges.

"They miss us, you know." It's Jan.

"I guess they do, so," Eddie agrees.

The door opens again and in walks a man with slick, combed-back hair. He wears a smart double-breasted suit and wire rimmed spectacles.

Eddie turns to him and smiles broadly. "How're you doing, Glen?"

The man returns his smile. "Good, Eddie."

Another man enters the room. He, too, is wearing spectacles.

"Bud," says Marilyn enthusiastically. "Please join us at the table. You too Glen."

The two men sit.

"We got six, a full house," says Eddie triumphantly. "Let's get this show on the road guys, and see what happens. I'm feeling lucky tonight. How about you guys? If we get through, we can serenade them. They'd like that."

The dark-haired man looks sceptical. "You really think it's gonna happen fellas?"

"Why wouldn't it?" Marilyn asks.

"Yeah, why wouldn't it?" Eddie chimes in. "Believe and achieve, that's the ticket."

"I just can't help believing you'll end up disappointed," dark hair cautions.

"Hey, come on now," Bud retorts. "You gotta have faith. If you don't, we got no chance of getting through."

"Yeah, Buddy's right," says Glen. "Show a little faith. Our friends miss us. We owe 'em. Vegas this place ain't, but we can still try to put on a show for the guys back home. Now what do you say?"

All eyes are on dark hair. He looks thoughtful. Finally, he grins and the tension eases.

"Okay, fellas," he says, allowing the grin to broaden, "I guess it's time to rock n roll."

With that, the six join hands and close their eyes, and dark hair asks the all important question; "Is anybody out there, on the other side of the tracks?"

WHO ARE YOU?

This morning starts much like any other. I get up and go
into the bathroom to shave. I've woken with a terrible
hangover, so I'm a little bit bleary-eyed. We've all been
there. It's the morning after the night before syndrome.
I feel like shit, but I've felt worse. Anyway, this morning
I'm in a rush. It's a week-day: I've got work to go to and
I've overslept, having forgotten to set the alarm because
I was so wrecked when I fell into my pit last night.
My girlfriend isn't there to wake me because I don't have
a girlfriend anymore. She abandoned me the week
before, citing unreasonable behaviour. Well, isn't that
just typical! She lives rent free in my apartment, spends
all my hard earned money, eats all my food, has an affair
with my best friend, and then she leaves me citing
unreasonable behaviour! Is it me or what?

So, I stagger into the bathroom feeling like I'm going
to die, and happen to glance in the mirror hanging above
the wash hand basin. Suddenly, I'm screaming the place
down, I'm so shocked by what I see.

"Arrgghhh! Oh my God, oh my God, no!"

And the reason for this great show of horrified
emotion? Well, the reflection in the mirror isn't mine! It's
somebody else staring back at me. The face bears not the
slightest resemblance to my own. The eyes are set wider

apart. The nose is broader and longer. The mouth is smaller, the lips rosier. Even the hair is different. It's longer and darker. I look away hoping and praying that when I look back I see someone I recognise, namely me, good old Jonny Franks. But when I do summon up the courage to do the deed, the shock only intensifies, because it's not me at all, it's the guy with the wide set eyes and the long dark hair.

I straighten up; move my head to the side. The unfamiliar reflection follows suit. I open my mouth, then snap it shut. The reflection does likewise and in perfect time.

"Shit!"

The reflection speaks the word in unison.

"Oh my God!"

And again!

I swallow and take a deep breath, and then I summon up the strength to speak the immortal words, "Who are you?" And guess what: the reflection asks the self-same question. Well, it would, wouldn't it. It's me, after all - only problem is, it doesn't look like me. But then, quite suddenly, reality changes again and the reflection speaks autonomously.

"Who are you?" it asks. It looks as shocked as I feel. It's as if it's seen me for the very first time, as if it's staring into a mirror from the reality of its own world to discover that horror upon horrors, its identity has been switched: seems like we're both suffering from a case of stolen identity.

Weird, man, weird!

The stranger in the mirror speaks again. "What are you doing in there? You're invading my space, mister.

Get out of there before I call the cops or—or something!"

Cops... Is he mental? He's the one who should be evicted if anyone should. He's in my mirror, for Chrissakes!

Or is he? The way he sees it, I'm in his. A case of perception is reality if ever there was one. But who's right? Maybe we both are? So, what do we do to resolve the problem amicably?

This calls for a cup of tea. So I leave the bathroom and go into the kitchen, put on the kettle and have a think. Hallucinated, maybe I hallucinated—it was a heavy night, after all. Yeah, that's it. No worries there, then.

When I finish drinking the tea, I return to the bathroom, my resolve strengthened, and force myself to look in the mirror again, hoping to see Jonny Franks instead of the smartass imposter. No such luck!

He's still there. I ask him his name. He asks me mine simultaneously. He's playing games. He's quite capable of speaking independently when he wants to. I already know that.

So, I give him what for: "Don't try to be a clever dick with me, mister! Tell me your ruddy name. At the same time you can damn well tell me what you want!"

Suddenly he's the one losing it and rages: "Enough! I've had enough of you, buster. You're nothing but a shitty little spirit. You think you own me but you don't, because you're dead! You don't even own your reflection, because you no longer have any substance. Now fuck off, Casper before I call in the ghost busters!"

"Huh?" What's he saying? That I'm a ghost? No way, Jose!

"Right, that does it!" I shout back. "Listen to me, you jumped up little twerp! This is what we're going to do. I'm going to give you the benefit of the doubt. We're going to sit down together and set this little episode to paper for posterity. And then we're going to go outside onto the street and stop the first person we see and ask them to describe our appearance. If their description matches you, I leave, if it's me; then you leave. Deal?"

He has a quick think and nods. "Deal."

So, we write it all down and go out onto the street and stop an old geezer with a walking stick and a little black dog.

"Describe my appearance," we say in unison.

He looks at us oddly, like he thinks we're mad or something, but in the end, he does as we ask.

That done, we go back to the apartment and into the bathroom and gaze at our reflection in the mirror. Up until then, I don't quite believe it, but when I see the man with the wide set eyes and long dark hair staring back at me, I finally have to. Back in the kitchen, we continue writing this literary masterpiece. And then we both sign it to say that we agree with the outcome of the exercise we've carried out involving the old man.

"I'll put the finishing touches to it afterwards," he says.

And then he signs his name, P Smith, and I sign mine, J Franks. What follows is the moment I've been dreading. I can barely bring myself to look. To my signature, he adds the word "deceased". Well, I have to take it on the chin, don't I? It seems that my girlfriend leaving me was the final straw.

When that part's all done, we leave the kitchen and return to the bathroom together for what will be the very last time. Once there, we take a deep breath, and look in the mirror at our reflection: correction, his reflection.

"Are you okay with this?" he asks.

What can I say? He's got me bang to rights.

I wink his eye at him and give him a cheeky little smile.

"I'll be seeing you, bucko."

That really makes him laugh. "Not if I see you first!"

END OF DAY

It's gone six, the department store is closed, and Tommy Drake is feeling nervous. As he rides the escalator to the building's upper level, he tries not to think about the dingy little room housing the store's outdated computer system. It's a cold, claustrophobic, remote place.

But he's got to go in there to do the end of day reports so he might as well get on with it. "Loony bin, Tommy, did you know this place used to be a loony bin?" Mac, the storeman told him today. That's the real reason he's feeling so reluctant to be here tonight.

As he passes row upon row of shadowy fixture stands he tries his best to relax. This evening is like any other, he tells himself. All he has to do is get the reports printed off, back them up on tape, jot down any points of concern in the diary and call the security guard so the day's takings can be counted in the strong room.

He enters the annex. Something makes him pause and glance back over his shoulder. It's a sound like a whisper. He scans the shadowy area, watchful. The fixtures look murky and distorted. He turns and is startled at the sight of his own reflection in a nearby mirror. A little further along, he stops again. He thinks he hears footsteps approaching from behind. When he looks no one is there, but he can sense a presence nevertheless. He wonders if a drunk or a dope-head is lurking somewhere out there in the darkness. He raises the two-way radio to his lips to call security down to take a look around, but then decides he is being foolish.

The toy department is silent as the grave. Then he's into ladies' fashion, where the mannequins stand like lost souls. Their presence gives him the jitters. It's the way they stare. He stares back, focusing on one in particular, observing its frozen expression and contrived posture. In the half-light the plaster cast model is undeniably creepy, and he averts his gaze. As he does so, the light plays a trick on his eyes. For one crazy moment, he is convinced the thing glances slyly at him. He looks warily at the others. They're like clones, lacking individuality. But that's not strictly true. The facial expressions differ. The difference is minute, but it's there.

He returns his attention to the first one. It's clothed in a slinky black off the shoulder number complimented by high-heeled shoes. The dark wig adorning its head is long and lustrous. The large vacant eyes are set in a delicately formed face. All of a sudden Tommy is captivated. If only she were real. He studies the expressionless eyes for movement, but they remain motionless and unseeing, and he continues on his way, suddenly worried about his state of mind.

He is finding it increasingly hard to cope. Karen is pregnant again, having assured him it couldn't happen. As if two young children aren't enough to deal with! Money worries dog them. How on earth will they survive? Sometimes he thinks he'll go crazy with the stress. He never wanted children in the first place, never really wanted marriage if the truth was known. He was happiest on his own, left to his own devices. And then he met Karen, and whatever Karen wanted, went, and suddenly his whole life changed: Karen who is so demanding, so controlling. And the children are suffocating him. He feels trapped. Maybe he'll end up mad like the residents of that asylum he's heard about.

His head is spinning. He feels unwell. It's the pressure: Karen and the blessed children. He wishes they would go away, that life, *his life*, could return to how it was before. Back then, it was so uncomplicated. Why had he allowed it to change? Karen and the kids are the reason he has to work back late. He is forced into having to process the end of day reports and cash reconciliation because of them. He is angry now, angry at the injustice of it all. He doesn't deserve the existence he has. It isn't fair.

He hurries through ladies' fashion wanting to be away from the mannequins, afraid to look back over his shoulder in case those cold lifeless eyes are scrutinising him. Had those dark frosty orbs really moved? Were they tracking his progress across the wide expanse of parquet floor at this very moment? If the mannequins did come to life, would they help or harm him? The hairs on the nape of his neck stiffen. He can sense the others watching him now. He wants to look around but doesn't dare for fear he might witness them advancing, taking stiff, uncoordinated, yet deliberate steps in his direction.

In the admin department, the silence is deathly. The lighting is virtually non-existent, making it difficult to see. He hurries out of there, goosed by the morbid atmosphere, turns a corner and walks straight into Charlie Gibson, the store's security guard. He jumps back in surprise, cursing beneath his breath.

Charlie looks amused. "What's wrong kid, seen a ghost?"

Tommy glances back over his shoulder, afraid he might see just that; or something worse, maybe. But the dimly lit corridor is deserted. What did he expect though? Did he really think he would see the mannequins standing there, possessed by the souls of the long dead asylum inmates? Was he crazy! What the hell had gotten into him to make him have such thoughts?

But then he thinks he hears a sound drift from that direction, resembling the click of high heels against a bare wooden floor, and his heart begins to race. He looks at Charlie, who talks with a phoney sounding Yank accent and claims to be a Vietnam Vet. Charlie is speaking, his speech a slow purposeful drawl. "We had this kid in our platoon. One morning he woke up with the same expression on his face as you have now. He looked haunted; like he'd seen his own destiny and was terrified by what he saw. Turns out he had good reason to look like that. You see, the Viet Cong liked to set booby traps for their enemies. A spiked ball on the end of a length of thick vine attached to a tree branch was a big favourite. It was triggered by movement: a man's foot touching the trip wire was usually enough to get things rolling..." Charlie allows the sentence to linger, appearing to draw pleasure from seeing the look of discomfort that has settled on the younger man's face.

Tommy, who has always disliked the security guard, suddenly decides he hates the man. He recalls his school days when there seemed to be a Charlie in every class he ever attended: some cretin who took pleasure in goading and taunting him to distraction, who picked on him mercilessly because he was weak and vulnerable, a natural victim. Nowadays there were two Charlie's in his life; the one standing before him and his dear, beloved wife who had forced her way into his quietly average existence, ruining it forever with her bullying nature. Oh, how he wished he could be rid of these people. Charlie's voice cuts into his thoughts.

"That kid in my platoon really did get the point, or should that be points? The spiked ball split his head like it was a watermelon. And believe me when I say he knew he had it coming. It was written all over his face as we left camp that morning. He just *knew*!"

Charlie breaks into an amused chuckle and wonders off along the corridor towards the annex, but then stops and turns, the good humour suddenly gone. That's the trouble with Charlie. He's unpredictable. "Radio me when you're ready to collect the money, kid. And don't take all night about it, or you'll find yourself wearing your ass for a face."

The threat is wasted. Tommy is thinking about the mannequins; imagining them wandering around out there, like murderous robots searching the store for a victim. With that thought in mind, he scurries away towards the end of day room, where it's cold and inhospitable, but where it's at least safe.

Once inside, he locks the door. As usual, an uncomfortable chill fills the room. It has to be that way because of the computer equipment. Against one wall stands an antiquated printer, the size of a large fridge. Throughout the night, long after Tommy is gone it will continue to print off reports. To its left, standing against the wall, sitting on top of an old desk, is the monitor linked to the master system, and a keyboard that will be used to key in the necessary commands to affect the end of day process. It is important the procedure is completed, otherwise the transaction registers will remain inoperable, and the store won't open for business the following day.

Tommy ensures there is enough paper available in the metal tray beneath the big old beast, so that all the reports can be printed off. Then he grabs the backup tapes off a shelf that stands above the master and slave consoles and slots the first into the master's back up drive. Like the printer, the computer hardware is outdated, but the store is struggling to meet budget, which means the business has to make do with what it's got. Tommy sets to work, but then pauses when he hears a gentle rap at the door. He turns towards the sound, listening hard.

"Is that you, Charlie?" he asks but there's no reply. He gets on the two-way. "Charlie, do you read me—over?"

The line crackles with the sound of static, but there's still no answer from Charlie. Tommy looks towards the door, his furtive imagination already coming up with a host of crazy scenarios. The soft slow rapping comes again. Fuck you, Charlie, he thinks angrily, fuck you and your stupid games. Suddenly, the big old printer springs to life with a thunderous clank, making Tommy jump - but at least the metallic chug of the outdated machine blocks out the unwanted sound from outside. Tommy tries the two-way again. This time, he doesn't mince his words.

"Charlie, if you're out there, answer me, you prick!"

All he gets for his trouble is the distorted crackle of static. He's just about to give up when Charlie's gravelly voice finally comes through.

"Who are you calling a prick, asshole?"

Tommy ignores the question and asks his own. "Where are you?"

"Third level, why?"

"What are you doing?"

"None of your damned business..."

"Charlie, this is serious."

"I'm checking the security breaker switch over in dinnerware if you must know. There was a problem but I think I've fixed it. Mind telling me what's up? You sound kinda strange."

"If what you say is true," says Tommy, "we've got an intruder in the store."

Charlie grunts and says he'll be right down.

Of course you will, thinks Tommy, convinced the guard is up to his usual juvenile tricks and is standing on the other side of the door. The printer continues doing its work, churning out an endless ream of paper filled with facts and figures. The computer screen goes momentarily blank and then another menu pops up. Tommy punches in the appropriate numbers and presses enter. He leaves his chair and ejects the first backup tape, swapping it for the next in the series. Going okay, he tells himself. Soon be out of here. Collect the money from the transaction safes, count the takings in the strong room, pop it into the safe and clock out. Easy fucking peasy...

The printer pauses again. Tommy hears the ominous rapping. Out of patience, he shouts, "Pack it in, Charlie or you'll get yourself reported!"

But it doesn't stop. Whoever is out there really is trying to upset his day. Tommy finally cracks. He rushes over to the door—is about to unlock it despite his reservations, when the two-way bursts back into life and

Charlie's voice is heard. He sounds perfectly natural but then again, old Charlie "I'm a big war hero" Gibson always does, even when he's secretly cracking up with the knowledge he's put another one over on poor Tommy Drake. Tommy demands to know where he is.

"Admin," says Charlie sounding as clear as a bell. Bet you are, thinks Tommy who by now has had enough of the charade. Ignoring his better judgment, he unlocks and opens the door in the sure knowledge that he'll find Charlie standing there with a great big stupid grin on his face. Sure enough, there is someone there.

Only it's not Charlie.

It's the mannequin. The one in the slinky dress and high-heels; and it's smiling. Understanding comes to Tommy in a blinding flash. When the figure before him turns and heads off along the corridor, he follows like a lamb to the slaughter. Only he isn't the one who will be slain, it's Charlie "I've seen a kid with an exploded head" Gibson who's going to get it, and Tommy, who somehow knows this without thinking about it, doesn't mind one little bit. In fact it seems only just. At last, a bully is about to get his comeuppance

They turn a corner and enter the main corridor. Tommy looks over the mannequin's shoulder and sees the security guard just ahead of him. Suddenly, Gibson's expression is filled with fear and incomprehension. He backs slowly away, but there's nowhere to go because unbeknown to him, more living mannequins are closing in from behind. Tommy watches them in fascinated disbelief. And then, quite suddenly, the smiling mannequin in the slinky black dress and high heels delivers a series of terrifying blows to Charlie's unprotected head using the heavy steel fixture arm it carries. Charlie screams once, very loudly, and falls back into the path of the others, and…

When it is all over and Charlie Gibson lies on the corridor floor with his head resembling that of the young soldier he spoke of earlier, Tommy returns to the small cramped room at the back of the store to complete the end of day process. When he's done that, he collects and counts the day's takings and reconciles the dockets.

He leaves the store wondering if Karen will scream like Charlie did when she answers the gentle rap at the door tonight.

Lightning Source UK Ltd.
Milton Keynes UK
UKOW04f1929130315

247870UK00001B/22/P

9 781908 596444